(#3)

EVERY DOG HAS HIS DAY

Bob Balaban

A Storyopolis Book

AN
APPLE
PAPERBACK

SCHOLASTIC INC.
New York Toronto London Auckland Sydney
Mexico City New Delhi Hong Kong Buenos Aires

For Owen and Ruby

No part of this publication may be reproduced in whole or in part, or stored in a retrieval system, or transmitted in any form or by any means, electronic, mechanical, photocopying, recording, or otherwise, without written permission of the publisher. For information regarding permission, write to Scholastic Inc., Attention: Permissions Department, 557 Broadway, New York, NY 10012.

ISBN 0-439-43456-4
Copyright © 2003 by Bob Balaban

All rights reserved. Published by Scholastic Inc.
SCHOLASTIC and associated logos are trademarks and/or registered trademarks of Scholastic Inc.

A Storyopolis Book
"Storyopolis, and the Storyopolis Skyline logo, are registered trademarks of Storyopolis Investment Corporation. All Rights Reserved. © SIC 1999."

12 11 10 9 8 7 6 5 4 3 2 1   3 4 5 6 7 8/0
                                                    40

Printed in the U.S.A.
First printing, September 2003

Contents

Praise for

"Balaban unleashes hilarious McGrowl. . . . Filled with absurd humor and fun, cartoonlike action."
— *USA Today,* review of
McGrowl #1: Beware of Dog

"Mr. Balaban takes his obvious love of language and wordplay and creates a magical tale of a mind-reading dog that all young minds should read. An intelligent and plentiful debut."
— *Jamie Lee Curtis*

"For anybody who has ever had a dog, loved a dog, or wanted a dog. A great adventure beautifully written. I hope Bob writes the next one about me."
— *Richard Dreyfuss*

CHAPTER ONE
Surprise!

McGrowl was finishing his second helping of egg foo yung and looking forward to a big bowl of green tea ice cream. Thomas's mother, Mrs. Wiggins, had cooked an authentic Chinese feast. She had even made fortune cookies. McGrowl sighed contentedly from his place of honor on the floor beside Thomas's chair. Little pots of yellow roses were arranged carefully along the meticulously set table. Mrs. Wiggins had put out her best china. Candles twinkled brightly. The dining room, she had to admit, had never looked better.

"Somebody's smacking their lips," Mrs. Wiggins said quietly. "And I wish they'd stop." McGrowl looked around to see who the offender was and realized it was none other than himself.

He swallowed delicately and attempted to wipe his muzzle on the kitchen towel Thomas had tied around his neck.

Good dog, Thomas thought. McGrowl received the telepathic message and sent back one of his own. He let Thomas know he thought it was unfair to expect proper table manners from a dog on his birthday.

McGrowl was exactly five years old today. To commemorate the joyous occasion he had received a shiny new Frisbee and the DVD of *Lassie Come Home*, his favorite movie. Thomas had attempted to surprise him, but since McGrowl could read his mind, this had been impossible.

Thomas looked over at his shaggy friend

and grinned. McGrowl was quietly licking specks of pork fried rice from the floor with his big pink tongue. His party hat had slipped over his eyes. Thomas reached down and tried to straighten it.

"Maybe he likes it that way," Thomas's older brother, Roger, whispered.

"Would anybody like to hear the rest of my story?" Mr. Wiggins asked peevishly. He was in the middle of another one of his long, boring anecdotes about something that had happened to him at work. He hated being interrupted.

"Children and dog, your father has something he wants to say. Listen up," Mrs. Wiggins announced as she clapped her hands several times. Even McGrowl stopped eating and looked up politely as Mr. Wiggins droned on about an "amazingly humorous incident" involving a new secretary and a fax machine.

Thomas's mind began to wander. Never in

his life did he imagine he would be celebrating his very own dog's birthday. First of all, his father was terrified of dogs and, second of all, his mother thought they messed up the house.

"More trouble than they're worth," she used to say. "Not to mention the added expense to the household budget. Dog food alone could set you back a fortune. And let's not forget about grooming and dental needs."

Of course, that was before McGrowl. In the ten short months since the dog had come to live at 27 Walnut Grove Avenue, Cedar Springs, Indiana 30022, Mrs. Wiggins had come to accept McGrowl as a member of the family.

Even Mr. Wiggins seemed to be getting used to him. He didn't exactly like McGrowl, but he wasn't exactly terrified of him, either. Thomas still couldn't believe his good fortune. If he hadn't been hunting for artifacts in the ravine that rainy Saturday afternoon almost one year ago, he might never have found his beloved pet.

And if it hadn't been raining that day, Mr. McCarthy's delivery truck wouldn't have skidded, McGrowl wouldn't have saved Thomas's life, and Mr. and Mrs. Wiggins would never have allowed the dog into their home in the first place.

Even if McGrowl hadn't had a run-in with an evil veterinarian and ended up with bionic superpowers, Thomas would have loved the dog. But it certainly was exciting having a golden retriever with a host of special abilities, including X-ray vision, the strength of a team of horses, and the ability to communicate telepathically.

"And then," Mr. Wiggins announced with a great flourish, "the entire box of paper fell onto the floor." Nobody was listening to a word he was saying. Even Mrs. Wiggins had begun to redecorate the living room in her mind. *Paint the rear wall hunter green, recover the ottoman . . .*

"Gotta run. Basketball practice starts early tonight." Roger was out of his chair and halfway across the room before Mrs. Wiggins could stop him.

"Not until we blow out the candles, young man. Where are your manners?" she said firmly. Roger returned dutifully to his seat. McGrowl didn't really mind. He knew Roger liked him. He also knew Roger only really cared about two things: playing basketball and spending time with his girlfriend, Alicia Schnayerson. In that order. Alicia was Violet's older sister. Violet was Thomas's best friend. The Schnayersons lived three houses down the block and across the street from the Wiggins family.

Mrs. Wiggins rang the little crystal bell Mr.

Wiggins had given her for their tenth anniversary. "If everybody's finished with their main course, let's clear the table and get ready for dessert."

Everyone hopped up and carried their plates into the kitchen. McGrowl grabbed his bowl in his mouth and started in as well. "The birthday dog gets to be waited on in this house," Thomas's mother said, taking the bowl from McGrowl. She gave him her cheeriest smile.

McGrowl experienced a warm glow of happiness from the tip of his floppy ears to the bottom of his bushy tail. How in the world did he ever get lucky enough to end up with a family like this?

McGrowl still missed his original owner, an elderly woman who had all but given up hope of ever seeing him again. The two had become separated when the woman became ill and had to be suddenly rushed to the hospital.

Even so, McGrowl had to admit that Thomas was the best boy a dog could ever dream of having.

Every night when he said his prayers, McGrowl was thankful for Thomas and his family. Then he would think about the old woman, who had since recovered and who missed the dog terribly. He wished he could tell her he was well and happy and hoped she was, too. He longed to introduce her to Thomas and tell her all about his exciting new life with the Wiggins family.

"Happy birthday to you" everyone sang as the kitchen door flew open. Mrs. Wiggins emerged carrying a big bowl of green tea ice cream. It was topped with flashing sparklers that spelled out McGrowl's name and the number five. Thomas took the bowl from his mother and put it on the floor near McGrowl.

The dog stood up immediately and stared at the bowl, lost in thought. "Isn't that adorable?" Mrs. Wiggins said. "He looks like he's making a wish." McGrowl looked over at Mrs. Wiggins, amazed. *Can she read my mind, too?* he wondered.

No, Thomas signaled McGrowl, *she can't.*

The dog closed his big brown eyes and wished with all his might. He wished for his boy to be happy and healthy. He wished for many more wonderful years with his new family. He wished for mashed potatoes at every meal. But most of all, he wished that the evil strangers who threatened to bring harm to Thomas and every resident of Cedar Springs would never return.

It had been months since their last visit. They had disguised themselves as a mayoral candidate and his lovely fiancée. They had gone by the names of Mel Muchnick and Lily Von Vleck, but their real names were Milton Smudge and Gretchen Bunting. And they had nearly succeeded in their vile plan to take over Cedar Springs and, eventually, the world. Thomas and McGrowl had thwarted them at the very last second.

McGrowl hoped he would recognize them the next time they surfaced. They were becoming more and more clever with their elaborate disguises. Only the distinct odor of sulfur and formaldehyde that oozed from every one of their pores could give them away. Both Smudge and Bunting had spent so many years doing bad things, they had begun to smell bad. As frequently a kind and gentle person will acquire a sweet and flowery scent, so will a truly evil person take on an acrid, pungent aroma.

McGrowl's sense of smell was extremely acute. It was one of his greatest assets. No amount of aftershave lotion or cheap French perfume had been able to cover up the telltale odor of Smudge and Bunting for very long. At least so far.

"Could someone please blow out the sparklers before the house catches on fire?" Mr. Wiggins said nervously. McGrowl took a deep breath and tried to blow. He didn't know that dogs are unable to expel air from their mouths the way people can. He was surprised when he opened his eyes and found the sparklers still sparkling away.

For a moment he considered turning around and expelling a different kind of air. Thomas issued an emphatic series of telepathic negatives. McGrowl got the point and barked loudly in the direction of the sparklers instead. They went out beautifully. He felt quite proud of himself until Roger declared, "I'm not eating any of that ice cream. It has dog breath all over it."

"Dog's breath is cleaner than people's breath — everybody knows that," said Thomas, rushing to McGrowl's defense.

"Well, don't you just know everything about everything." Roger was pretty touchy about anything even remotely related to biology. He was currently scraping by with a D, and he wasn't very happy about it.

"Don't fight, kids. This is a happy occasion," Mrs. Wiggins said firmly. The two brothers just glared at each other. "First one to make up doesn't have to take out the trash."

"Sorry," Roger blurted. "Can I go now?" And he bolted from the table. But not before leaning over and patting McGrowl. "Didn't mean to criticize your breath, pal. You're a good dog." McGrowl looked up gratefully. Thomas was grateful as well.

"Thanks, Rog," he said quietly.

Mrs. Wiggins spooned heaps of green tea ice cream into dishes and passed out the fortune cookies she had made. She gave McGrowl a double helping of ice cream. He thumped his powerful tail happily. Thomas sent him a message reminding him not to dent the floor.

"Looks like I'll be doing some traveling," Mr. Wiggins chortled as he opened his fortune cookie and read the little scrap of paper inside: "'Take your wife on a much-needed vacation. Soon.'" Mrs. Wiggins didn't just make the *cookies*, she made the fortunes as well.

She opened her cookie and cheerfully read: "'Treat yourself to a manicure and a facial. Your husband won't mind.'" Mr. Wiggins smiled broadly. "Why, honey, thank you," Mrs. Wiggins said, and kissed her husband on the top of his shiny bald head.

"Doesn't McGrowl want to read his fortune?" she asked.

Thomas ripped open McGrowl's cookie. A neatly folded fortune fell to the table. Thomas picked it up and prepared to read it. McGrowl had recently perfected his reading skills and could have done the job himself, but Thomas and Violet had made a pact never to let anyone know about the dog's special abilities.

Thomas read the fortune and turned pale. McGrowl read the boy's mind and turned paler. The fortune said: "You and that dreadful boy of yours are in great danger, and there is absolutely nothing you can do about it." It was signed "Frighteningly yours, Milton Smudge."

How did it get there? Where was Smudge? When did he return? Was he lurking somewhere about the house? McGrowl scanned the area with his superhearing.

"What's the matter, honey? Aren't you going to read us McGrowl's fortune?" Mrs. Wiggins looked at Thomas expectantly. Mr. Wiggins chimed in: "Cat got your tongue?"

Thomas couldn't read that fortune out loud. His parents would have been too upset. And as the message said, there was absolutely nothing they could do about it. His mind was racing. What would his mother have written? "'You will soon be eating a lot of peanut butter,'" Thomas suddenly exclaimed.

"That's funny," she replied, "I don't remember writing anything like that. Let me see, sweetie." She leaned over, about to take the fortune out of Thomas's hands. But just then McGrowl looked up, grabbed the fortune in his teeth with lightning speed, and swallowed it whole.

"You'd think he'd had enough to eat already, what with two helpings of egg foo yung and that enormous portion of ice cream," Mr. Wiggins ventured suspiciously. He was always on the lookout for erratic behavior on McGrowl's part.

Mr. Wiggins still believed that dogs were wild animals, never to be trusted. "Guess I'll retire to the den and watch a little evening news," he said, a little too casually. Then he was off like a shot.

"All right, honey," Mrs. Wiggins called out. McGrowl innocently picked up his new Frisbee and begged Thomas to throw it to him. "Not in the house, kids," she warned.

"Okay, Mom," Thomas said. He picked up

the trash bag from the kitchen, then he and the dog ran to the back door.

"Happy birthday, McGrowl," Mrs. Wiggins called as she made her way to the kitchen. "Remember to wipe those paws when you're finished playing." She gave McGrowl a friendly little wave and disappeared around the corner.

She would do the dishes, mop the floor until it glowed, and polish every piece of silver before she put it away. Then she would retire to the den to sew more name tags on Thomas's clothes.

Thomas's class was about to leave for Wilderness Weekend, the annual fifth-grade trip to Devil's Island in nearby Lake Wappinger. He had been talking about the event since first grade. He had been dreaming about it since second. Now the big weekend had finally arrived, and all he could think about was the unsettling message inside McGrowl's fortune cookie.

EVERY DOG HAS HIS DAY

Thomas and McGrowl threw the Frisbee until there wasn't a scrap of light outside and Mrs. Wiggins made them come in. All the while they watched and waited and listened for signs of the evil stranger. They found no evidence of anything suspicious. All the houses on the block exuded friendliness and a cozy sense of security.

But there was evil in the air. McGrowl was certain of it. A new adventure was about to begin, and Thomas and McGrowl would not rest easy until it was over. This was one birthday neither of them was likely to forget for quite some time.

CHAPTER TWO
Ready, Set, Go!

Thomas and McGrowl waited patiently outside Violet's house. Violet wasn't late. They were twenty minutes early. Neither of them had slept a wink the night before. All they could think about was that fortune cookie. By the time the sun finally peeked through the curtains and Thomas's alarm rang, the boy was already washed and dressed, and McGrowl had sniffed every corner of the house twice. He didn't detect one single molecule of formaldehyde.

Violet appeared at the door.

"It's forty-one degrees out there, young lady. Put on socks," Mrs. Schnayerson called out.

"Uh-oh," Violet muttered under her breath. She hated wearing socks and only put them on when she absolutely had to. She claimed they made her toes feel funny.

Violet's mother stood, arms folded, beside her in the doorway. "I'm waiting." She tapped her foot impatiently against the wooden floor of the porch. Thomas wondered if Mrs. Schnayerson had been taking lessons from his mother.

At last Violet was out the door, socks firmly in place and pigtails freshly braided. McGrowl thought they would never get going. He couldn't wait for Thomas to tell Violet about the message from the evil stranger.

"Did you save the fortune?" Violet asked, wide-eyed. "Maybe there were fingerprints." By now the three friends were halfway to school. They had decided to walk. The chances of having a private conversation on the overcrowded little bus that took them to the Stevenson School every morning were minimal. McGrowl walked several steps ahead and scanned the neighborhood for anything out of the ordinary. So far, so good.

"McGrowl ate it," Thomas replied.

"The cookie?" Violet asked.

"The fortune," Thomas said, and looked around suspiciously. He pulled his wind-breaker up around his neck. The air was crisp and cool. The sun was shining brightly. The smell of burning leaves and newly mowed lawns filled the air. It was a perfect autumn day — if you didn't have an evil stranger and his accomplice to think about.

"Say, did you guys finish that history as-signment?" Lenny Winkleman ran up and asked nervously. "Didn't you think twenty-seven pages was sort of, you know, unfair?" As he spoke he chewed on a raggedy fingernail. Lenny was very tall and very skinny. He was always worrying about something. If it hadn't been last night's homework, it would have been tomorrow's lunch.

"It's not due until next Thursday," Violet replied tersely. She didn't want to be rude, but she hoped he would go away.

"I'm relieved," Lenny said. He didn't look relieved. He shifted his weight awkwardly from one foot to the other. "If it rains today, think we'll have soccer anyway?" he said, looking up at the perfectly blue sky. "I may be getting a cold."

"Who knows?" Violet murmured.

"If I get sick, my mom's not letting me go on Wilderness Weekend," Lenny said forlornly. "You guys got your stuff together?"

Lenny had Velcroed himself onto Thomas and Violet as usual. So much for their private conversation. They gave in and talked about

Wilderness Weekend. McGrowl listened intently. Although pets were strictly forbidden, he had to admit the event sounded like a lot of fun.

The group would be divided into two teams, the Browns and the Greens. Everyone would spend the weekend living in "Conditions of Yesteryear," as posters all over Thomas's homeroom proudly announced. The teams would compete in events like getting water to boil without using matches and putting up a tent without using any tools. Points would be awarded for just about anything, including fewest mosquito bites, best table manners, and Thomas's personal favorite, keeping a Life Saver in your mouth the longest without dissolving or breaking it.

Days would be spent gathering edible nuts and berries, and at night, everyone would sit around a campfire and tell stories. That is, if they could ever get the fire to light.

Warm clothing and blankets were recommended, but campers were told to leave behind anything modern. No flashlights, no CD players, and no cell phones or pagers. If a Native American didn't have it two hundred years ago, you couldn't bring it.

"My mom tried to make me pack Band-Aids, but I wouldn't do it. Think I should reconsider?" Lenny asked anxiously.

Before Thomas had a chance to reply, they arrived at school and were joined by a crush of students getting out of cars and vans and buses. The Stevenson School was made up of three tightly clustered redbrick buildings: lower school on the right, middle school on the left, and high school in the center. The three divisions arrived at exactly the same time. Morning rush was so noisy you could barely hear yourself think.

McGrowl spotted Lewis Musser, the class bully, sauntering by. The dog quickly alerted Thomas, who nudged Violet. They managed to avoid Lewis by dropping some pencils and bending to pick them up.

Stuart Seltzer, the best science student in the entire lower school, wasn't so lucky. Lewis cornered him halfway down the hallway and extracted two dollars, Stuart's math homework, and several pieces of bubble gum.

"Pay ya back Monday, Stuey," Lewis said casually, and hurried off to bother someone else. He knew Stuart hated to be called Stuey. He didn't care.

Then the bell rang, and everyone raced into their homerooms to take their seats.

McGrowl walked around to the back of the building to wait for recess. He was the only dog allowed on school grounds. He had endeared himself to Mr. Postino, the custodian, by helping to clean up after assembly and making sure none of the students walked on the newly seeded lawn in front of the middle school.

EVERY DOG HAS HIS DAY

"Happy campers," Miss Thompson chirped from her desk at the front of the classroom, "you are about to embark on the adventure of your lives." Everyone tried not to laugh. In preparation for the trip to Devil's Island, Thomas's homeroom teacher had come to school dressed in full Wilderness Weekend attire.

She had on a woven straw cap with several large feathers hanging off it, a blouse decorated with pictures of leaves and birds, and enormous purple galoshes.

As she spoke she made sweeping gestures with her spindly arms. "Oh, the joys you shall experience!" Her eyes misted over, and she dabbed at them with a lace hanky. "To camp outside under the stars . . . to consume nuts and berries as our ancestors did in days of old . . ." One of the feathers that dangled from her hat kept getting in her mouth. She tried to swat it away.

Violet caught Thomas's eye for a second and immediately spotted the twinkle that meant a laugh wasn't far behind. It made her want to giggle. She looked away quickly.

"On a more serious note," Miss Thompson continued, "in the event you encounter poison ivy on the island . . ." The teacher stopped speaking. The tip of another one of the feathers lodged itself inside the corner of her mouth. She flicked it away and continued. "Flood the affected area of your skin with cold water immediately." The feather fluttered back into her mouth.

"Miss Thompson, Miss Thompson," Lenny Winkleman called out as he raised his hand frantically.

"What's the matter, Lenny?" the teacher asked patiently.

"You have a feather in your mouth, Miss Thompson." Lenny said.

"Yes, I know, Lenny," she said, jamming the

feather back into its place on the brim of her hat.

She would never have admitted it, but Miss Thompson hated going on Wilderness Weekend. She had hated it ever since she came to teach at the Stevenson School seventeen long years ago. She hated sleeping in a tent. She hated the bugs. She hated the lack of hot water. But most of all, she hated the snakes.

It didn't matter that the only snakes found on Devil's Island were small and green and utterly harmless. The mere thought of slimy reptiles was enough to make Miss Thompson's eyes bulge and her heart pound.

In fact, at that moment she happened to recall a particularly large snake she had recently seen on a class trip to the zoo. She gave an involuntary shudder that dislodged the feather from her hat altogether. It fell to the floor, brushing against her leg along the way.

She mistook the feather for a snake and immediately screamed and jumped on top of her desk. "Snake! Help!" she hollered, and danced around wildly.

The entire class sat stunned. Miss Thompson was known for her poise and quiet dignity. And there she was, dressed in an outlandish outfit, standing on her desk, screaming at the top of her lungs. Violet let loose with a whooping, uncontrollable laugh. Thomas and the rest of the class joined in.

"What, boys and girls, may I ask, is so funny?" Miss Thompson demanded in a shrill, nasal voice. As soon as the words were out of her mouth, she looked down at herself and realized how ridiculous she looked. Then she started laughing along with everybody else.

McGrowl watched from his place outside the window. He cocked his head to one side and listened intently. School certainly seemed like a lot of fun.

At last Miss Thompson calmed down, removed her hat, put the feather in a drawer, and started acting like a teacher again. She reminded everyone never to stand under a tree in a rainstorm. She recommended using garlic as a natural insect repellent and dried mud as sunscreen. She urged the students to have their parents sew name tags on everything.

In Thomas's case, the reminder was hardly necessary. Mrs. Wiggins had been staying up late for days, making sure that no item of Thomas's clothing would remain unlabeled. Roger joked that their mother would have sewn name tags on Thomas's tissues, if she could find the time.

Lenny Winkleman's hand shot up again. "Will there be soap on the island?"

"Like, if there wasn't soap, maybe we would all die or something," Lewis grumbled.

"That is not a nice thing to say, Lewis

Musser," Miss Thompson said sternly. She really wished that boy would learn to behave himself. "Soap was used by Native Americans, class," Miss Thompson continued. "So we'll have plenty of it on our trip."

"That's great," Lenny replied earnestly. "Because I'm highly susceptible to germs, and if I don't wash my hands regularly, I tend to get really sick." He aimed the second half of his remark squarely over at Lewis, as if Lewis cared one single bit. Lewis was about to make another rude remark, but Miss Thompson cut him off swiftly with one of her famous impossible questions.

"What substance beginning with the letter *s* formed the primary ingredient for all soap used prior to the nineteenth century?" She searched the room for a raised hand. No one had the slightest idea. Not even Stuart Seltzer, who prided himself on his vast knowledge of obscure details about nature.

McGrowl, however, had recently observed an eighth-grade class on the history of the American family. So he just happened to know the answer. He beamed the word *suet* quickly to Thomas.

Thomas raised his hand and gave the correct answer, much to Miss Thompson's surprise and delight. Violet gave Thomas a knowing look. Thomas hoped Miss Thompson wouldn't ask him what suet was.

Next came math, followed by a history class that Thomas thought would never end. Poor Lenny Winkleman discovered he had completed the wrong assignment and was unable to answer a single question on the pop quiz. He nearly hyperventilated and had to be sent to Nurse Boynton's office, where he spent the remainder of the day blowing into a paper bag.

At last the bell for recess rang and everyone ran screaming and yelling out to the playground. McGrowl joined Thomas and Violet and several other fifth-graders in a lively game of kickball. Ralph Sidell, the best athlete in the lower school, sent a ball flying over the back fence. McGrowl went racing after it, and with a masterful leap backward into the air managed to catch it in his teeth. He returned, holding the ball proudly in his mouth. It was then that he noticed the man.

Gosling Fletch, the new head of the high school science department, came running out of the biology lab and across the playground. His loose-fitting laboratory coat flapped wildly in the breeze. The enormously tall, skinny teacher clutched a beaker in one hand and a Bunsen burner in the other. His hair was long and unruly, and he looked upset.

Thomas and Violet noticed him a second later. McGrowl hurried over and took a discreet sniff at the ground upon which the man had just scurried. There was no question about it. The man's footprints fairly reeked of formaldehyde. Had Milton Smudge returned in the guise of Gosling Fletch? It seemed a distinct possibility.

CHAPTER THREE
Close Call

Thomas, Violet, and McGrowl decided to use the rest of their recess time to pay a visit to the chemistry lab. McGrowl entered first. The room was empty. A dozen desks fitted with beakers, Bunsen burners, and sinks were lined up neatly on the perimeter of the classroom. The bell for the next period wouldn't ring for several minutes, and Gosling Fletch was nowhere to be seen.

McGrowl sent Thomas a message telling him the coast was clear. Thomas tiptoed in and started searching the room. Violet stayed outside to stand guard in case Fletch arrived early. She looked anxiously down at her watch. Eleven minutes until next period. "Please hurry," she whispered to no one in particular.

The first thing Thomas noticed was how clean everything was. Even though seventeen tenth-graders had just finished dissecting seventeen earthworms, every desk was spotless, and the floor looked as though it had just been freshly scrubbed.

McGrowl sniffed about excitedly. The faint odor of formaldehyde was everywhere. He poked his nose into every corner and cubby. It was Thomas who noticed the brown lunch bag first. It stared up at him, innocently, from the bottom of a wastebasket. He reached in to pick it up. McGrowl sent a telepathic message. *Be careful.* Thomas was grateful for the warning. Perhaps the crumpled paper sack was a trap of some kind.

Thomas laid the bag on the floor. McGrowl

came over and looked into it with his X-ray vision. Satisfied they were in no immediate danger, he poked at it with his paws. With the delicacy of a skilled surgeon, McGrowl opened the bag, gave it a good sniff, and declared the contents safe. He telepathically instructed Thomas to remove several neatly wrapped objects.

First, there emerged an apple core, followed by some stale crusts of bread and a bit of dried brown dough.

"I think it's some kind of cookie," Thomas said. "What do you think, McGrowl? Ever seen anything like it before?"

McGrowl raised his eyebrows and leaned over to sniff. *What a delicious aroma,* the dog thought. *Almonds mixed with sugar . . . and just a hint of vanilla extract.* His mouth began to water. He nearly forgot the seriousness of the situation and almost ate the cookie.

Then McGrowl returned to his senses. This

was no ordinary cookie — this was a clue. Closer inspection revealed that it was a piece of a fortune cookie. McGrowl focused his powerful vision on the cookie shard. It appeared to have been homemade. Thorough molecular analysis determined that the cookie was created from precisely the same ingredients Thomas's mother had used in her own fortune cookies.

What was Gosling Fletch doing with one of Thomas's mother's homemade cookies? Thomas had a feeling he knew the answer, and it gave him a queasy feeling in the pit of his stomach.

"What do we do now?" Thomas wondered. Before McGrowl had a chance to reply, Violet's voice rang out from her post outside the chemistry lab.

"Why, hello, Mr. Fletch," she said a little too loudly. "I was hoping you could tell me if earthworms really do regenerate."

Quickly, Thomas repacked the contents of the bag and hid it under his shirt. He and Mc-Growl looked around for a place to hide. Meanwhile, Violet desperately tried to buy them a little more time.

"You see," she continued, "I keep several of them as pets, and one of them seems to have lost his head. Or his tail. I'm not really sure which." As she spoke, she wrung her hands, and her voice trembled. She was giving one of her finest performances. "I've become extremely attached to it. I call it Seymour." She nearly managed to squeeze out a tear or two.

"Strange," Fletch murmured. He brushed past Violet and entered the lab. She rushed in after him. "You appear," the teacher continued, "to have developed a great deal of feeling for a creature incapable of returning affection." As he spoke he looked around the room suspiciously. "You might consider hamsters. Or a lovely little white mouse."

And then he noticed the empty wastebasket. He leaned over, peered into it, and scratched his head. "I could swear . . ." he began.

"But aren't hamsters difficult to train?" Violet asked insistently. She had noticed the door to the broom closet ajar and a wisp of golden tail sticking out.

"Have you ever tried to train an *earthworm*?" the teacher responded archly. "The mind fairly boggles at the thought."

Just then the door to the broom closet flew open, and Thomas came tumbling out. He had been hiding inside, standing on top of a large bucket in an attempt to make room for McGrowl. He lost his balance, tried to grab on to the door, and flew through the air. He landed right at Mr. Fletch's large feet.

"What is going on here?" the teacher demanded in a booming voice. Thomas opened his mouth. Nothing emerged but a faint squeak. Perhaps it was the ferocious glare from Mr. Fletch, who had pulled himself up to his full height of nearly seven feet.

Or perhaps it was the deep-set ridges that cut a jagged path across the man's strangely wide forehead. Violet raced to think of something to say. "Well, my friend, uh, was looking for . . . uh, I don't really remember, actually . . . but it was quite important . . . hmm . . ."

At last, Thomas found his voice. "What she's trying to say . . ." he began, and was immediately interrupted when McGrowl dashed madly out of the closet, ran for the door, and headed across the courtyard in front of the science building. He darted this way and that, doing his best to give the impression of a runaway dog.

"Quick, don't let him escape!" Violet shouted, knowing perfectly well that McGrowl would never try to run away. The dog was merely providing the children with an excuse to bolt. In a flash, the two children were out the door and racing after McGrowl. Mission accomplished.

Mr. Fletch watched and considered joining in the chase, but the bell rang and his thoughts quickly turned to coping with the next seventeen boisterous students who were currently tumbling into his classroom. He would attend to Thomas, Violet, and the peculiar yellow dog later.

In the rush, the brown lunch bag containing what might be a significant clue had fallen from its hiding place under Thomas's shirt. It lay on the ground outside of the chemistry lab, concealed by a patch of tall grass. At least for the time being.

CHAPTER FOUR
Dark Shadows

Violet and Thomas were leaving fifth-period history class. They were heading to sixth-period assembly when Sophie Morris came running by, waving her arms and shouting, "Do *not* go to assembly, I repeat, do *not* go to assembly."

Sophie absolutely loved issuing orders and was something of a teacher's pet. She was always the first to volunteer for eraser-cleaning duty, and she brought an endless supply of apples to each of her teachers on a daily basis.

She continued yelling at the top of her lungs,

"Go to the library instead. We're having a Wilderness Weekend meeting there with Pop Wheeler. Pass it on!" Then she flew off to tell everyone else she could find. Her tiny loafers clattering across the hallway sounded like a troop of ponies.

There was simply no doubt about it. Pop was Stevenson's favorite teacher. He was known for his sound but folksy advice on just about any subject, and he always had time for a student in need. He was the leader and chief organizer of Wilderness Weekend, and he taught shop to the middle and lower schools.

There was nothing Pop couldn't do with a saw and a hammer and a rasp. He had made the little birdhouses that decorated the playground. He could whittle a reasonable facsimile of a cardinal, the state bird of Indiana, in less than a minute. Now he had scheduled an emergency seminar to review special survival skills.

Pop's adorable wife, Mamie, always accompanied Pop on Wilderness Weekend. While on Devil's Island, she was in charge of cooking, cleaning, and tending to the occasional skinned knee or bruised ego. She was an equally beloved teacher at Stevenson, but no one ever listened to any of her advice.

Mamie taught middle school home economics, and she was as flaky as her piecrusts. Nothing she cooked ever turned out properly. Her soufflés didn't rise, her puddings had lumps the size of golf balls, and her angel food cake was unlikely to be described as heavenly.

She never went anywhere without her gingham apron. Mamie was plump and jolly, and she always smelled as if she had just been baking cinnamon buns, which, indeed, she usually had. "There is nothing a cinnamon bun can't cure," she was known to say, "except a life-threatening disease."

Then Pop would say that Mamie's cinnamon

buns *were* a life-threatening disease. Like the rest of Mamie's creations, her cinnamon buns were usually inedible. And then the two of them would laugh until their ample bellies shook. Recently, several mice had, in fact, taken seriously ill upon eating a discarded batch.

And yet there was always a waiting list to get into Mamie's classes. No one ever followed her recipes, but everyone loved her sense of humor and cheery optimism.

When Sophie Morris had herded the last stray fifth-grader into the library, Pop Wheeler addressed the eager crowd. "Okay, kids," he began, "you're on Devil's Island, it's late at night, you're in your bedroll, and you spot a bear heading toward you." Thirty eager children sat, transfixed. "Quick, what d'ya do?"

Hands flew up all over the room. "Stuart Seltzer." Pop pointed to the excited youngster in the front row. "If you waved any harder, you'd take off like a helicopter. Out with it, son."

"I'd lie right down and pretend to be dead and the bear wouldn't eat me because bears only eat live food," Stuart Seltzer answered briskly. There was no question that Stuart knew a lot about furbearing animals of the forest.

A hush fell over the room. Stuart's classroom comments were frequently accompanied by some form of stunned silence. He had recently delivered an oral report entitled "One Hundred Little-known Facts About Raccoons" in which he exploded forever the myth that these cute little mammals washed their food because they were clean.

"No," he had said emphatically, "the clever raccoon dips its food in water because it has no saliva glands and cannot swallow without the addition of moisture." He had received an A+.

"Well, young Mr. Seltzer," Pop said, "on Devil's Island, what you do if you see a bear is you have your eyes examined, because there is not one single bear in the entire place." He broke into a grin from ear to ear and then exclaimed, "Trick question!"

The class laughed, visibly relieved. Pop continued. "You might find a chipmunk. And I saw a rabbit there once. But a bear? 'Fraid not, Stuart. Good answer, though." Pop had a way of saying you were wrong without making you feel bad.

McGrowl was sitting patiently outside the window when he heard rustling leaves and immediately noticed a familiar pungent odor. He leaped to attention. Gosling Fletch stood hovering in the shadows, near the entrance to the library, waiting for the meeting to come to an end. McGrowl beamed an urgent message to Thomas, who passed the news along to Violet.

Then Pop Wheeler reminded the happy campers that the bus was leaving tomorrow morning at eight o'clock on the dot. The trip would last from Saturday to Monday afternoon, and each day would be packed with activities.

"So for heaven's sake, get a good night's sleep, campers," Pop warned. "Points will be deducted for yawning."

Lenny's hand shot up. "I suffer from a condition called sleep apnea and sometimes I wake up a lot so I might not get a good night's rest which might cause me to yawn the next day but it wouldn't really be my fault. Will that be taken into consideration?" Lenny's words tumbled out in one long, anxious gulp.

"Only kidding, son, only kidding." Pop chuckled. As he distributed a printed sheet of last-minute reminders, Pop noticed something out the window. "Say, wait a minute, what's that out there?"

Had Pop seen Gosling Fletch? Violet and Thomas turned quickly to look. But Fletch was nowhere to be seen. Instead, Pop ran to the window and pointed directly at McGrowl. Mamie joined him, and they both peered out. "What an adorable wolf," she said. Mamie was not only a terrible cook, she was notoriously nearsighted.

Pop just chuckled. "That is one of the finest examples of a golden retriever I've ever seen." McGrowl's chest swelled with pride. "Say, who belongs to that fine animal?" Pop asked.

A loud chorus of "Thomas, Thomas" resounded throughout the room.

"I certainly hope you'll be bringing that dog to Devil's Island, young man," Pop said.

"No pets allowed on Wilderness Weekend," Sophie Morris interjected solemnly. She had wanted to bring along her poodle, Fluffy, and knew the rules regarding pets only too well.

"Surely, we could make an exception in the case of . . . what do you call him?" Pop asked.

"McGrowl," Thomas proudly replied. "He'd love to come. Wouldn't you, boy?"

McGrowl put his paws on the window ledge and barked happily.

"Look how intelligent you are, fella," Pop said cheerfully. "I bet you'd be a big help on the island. Do you like to fetch?" Pop opened the window, leaned out, and ruffled McGrowl's fur.

"This isn't fair," Sophie protested. "Fluffy gets to go, too."

"Tell you what, Sophie Morris," Pop said patiently, "this year McGrowl gets to go on Wilderness Weekend, next year Fluffy gets to go on the sixth grade's annual trip to the state capital, Indianapolis Adventures?"

"Okay," said Sophie. She seemed pleased with the compromise. Thomas and McGrowl were thrilled.

Then the meeting was over. Thomas and Violet managed to sneak out a side door, successfully avoiding Mr. Fletch. They joined

McGrowl and raced to the bus stop. As soon as they arrived, Mr. Fletch spotted them and ran toward them, screaming, "Stop, little children. Stop!"

The bus arrived in the nick of time, and Thomas, Violet, and McGrowl quickly boarded just as Gosling Fletch arrived, disheveled and panting. The bus pulled away, and the children looked back nervously and watched Mr. Fletch waving the brown paper lunch bag in the air, pointing at it emphatically and yelling something they couldn't quite make out.

Fletch must have found it on the ground where Thomas had dropped it. That meant he knew Thomas had discovered the fortune cookie and was onto his true identity. Thomas's heart sank. Slowly, an odd-looking woman emerged from behind a large bush and stood beside Mr. Fletch. She tugged at his arm and whispered furiously. She was short and round and appeared to be wearing a false nose.

Oh, no, Thomas thought. *Gretchen Bunting is short and round. The evil stranger's accomplice has returned as well.*

But then he had a comforting thought. Tomorrow morning, he, Violet, and McGrowl would board the bus for Wilderness Weekend. It would carry them far away from the malevolent Mr. Fletch and his partner in crime. No harm would come to them on Devil's Island. Pop and Mamie Wheeler would see to that.

All they had to do was make it through the night.

CHAPTER FIVE
Puppy Love

Thomas and McGrowl arrived home safely. McGrowl immediately did a thorough search of the premises. In the time it took Thomas to hang up his hat and coat, the dog checked out not only upstairs and downstairs but the front and backyards, the crawl space under the house, and the garage as well.

No signs of any evil strangers so far. Then the doorbell rang. Thomas's heart began to pound. He took a quick look through the peephole and, much to his relief, spotted Violet's older sister, Alicia, and her hyperactive little dog, Miss Pooch.

Before the door was even halfway open, Miss Pooch became so excited at the sight of McGrowl, she started leaping up and down frantically and making high-pitched yelping noises.

"I hope you don't mind, but . . . No, Miss Pooch, no . . ." Alicia struggled to restrain her dog, who was busy scrambling up one of her legs. "I mean, I asked Roger to check with you guys . . . and he said it was okay with you, but . . . Heel, Miss Pooch, heel!" Alicia was practically yelling now. "I don't know, is it *really* okay? I mean, be honest, now . . . *really*?" Alicia implored.

Thomas had absolutely no idea what she was talking about. As usual, Roger had completely forgotten to ask Thomas whatever it was he was supposed to ask. Alicia explained that she and her parents had to attend a family wedding in Livingston, Indiana, and they desperately needed someone to take care of Miss Pooch. Violet would be staying home tonight with a baby-sitter, but the woman was allergic to dogs.

"Just until Monday. She won't be any trouble at all," Alicia said, attempting to clutch the wriggling dog tightly to her. "I brought over her food and a favorite toy."

She pointed at the little overnight bag hanging from her shoulder, into which Miss Pooch was now attempting to claw her way. "I don't know what's gotten into her," Alicia said. "She's usually so well behaved." This was a lie. Miss Pooch had flunked out of dog obedience school three times.

Before Thomas had a chance to reply, Miss Pooch pried herself loose from Alicia's grasp and started running madly around the hallway. She was madly in love with McGrowl and was doing everything in her power to attract his attention. She skittered across the room. The area rug that covered the parquet floor went flying and nearly careened into the stairs. One of Mrs. Wiggins's precious antique vases teetered on the three-legged table beneath which the dog ultimately slid to a stop. She looked coyly back at McGrowl, but he merely yawned and looked away, uninterested.

"Calm down, Miss Pooch," Alicia warned, "or Thomas and McGrowl won't be willing to baby-sit for you this weekend."

"We'll be away at Wilderness Weekend with Violet," Thomas reminded Alicia. "But maybe my parents can keep an eye on Miss Pooch."

McGrowl breathed a sigh of relief. He eyed Miss Pooch warily and wished she would go away. Meanwhile, Roger, the source of all the confusion, was conveniently missing. He was spending the weekend at a basketball retreat.

Miss Pooch was a bulldog-Chihuahua mix,

a "bullwawa," as Alicia referred to her. She had fluffy brown-and-white fur, an impish face, and an undershot jaw from which protruded a crowded row of sharp little teeth.

Alicia thought Miss Pooch looked adorable. McGrowl thought she resembled a piranha. Ever since moving in with the Wigginses, he had gone to great lengths to stay away from the ill-tempered little creature.

Suddenly, the front door flew open and Mrs. Wiggins came hurrying in, carrying a load of groceries. "Hi, Alicia. Hello there, Miss Pooch. Did we remember to wipe our messy little feet on the mat?" she asked as she quietly took in the mangled area rug and did her best to retain her composure. Mrs. Wiggins liked everything in her house to be neat and tidy at all times. "Anybody want to help me unpack?"

Everyone helped Thomas's mom into the kitchen with her packages. Everyone, that is, except Miss Pooch, who ran around in tight little circles and occasionally tried to jump up and grab food from the tops of the grocery bags with her razorlike teeth. Then Alicia ran off to pack for the wedding.

"Thanks so much, Mrs. Wiggins," she called out. By the time Thomas's mother replied with a quizzical "For what?" Alicia was already well out of earshot.

"For dog-sitting Miss Pooch this weekend," Thomas said.

"Oh, no," said Mrs. Wiggins. "What will your father say?"

Just then, Mr. Wiggins's car pulled up, and McGrowl took matters into his own hands. Bad behavior in the home of his beloved family was not to be tolerated. He quickly cornered Miss Pooch, barked sternly, and let her know in no uncertain terms who was top dog in the house. She rolled obediently onto her back and demonstrated complete submission. For about a second.

Then Miss Pooch jumped to her feet, ran over to McGrowl, licked him right on the nose, and started dancing around joyously. Poor McGrowl. He was so embarrassed he would have crawled under the rug if it wasn't already lying in a heap at the bottom of the stairs.

The door flew open again, and Mr. Wiggins came rushing into the house, carrying an artfully decorated cheese platter arranged to depict a winter wonderland scene. Hundreds of carefully molded cheese balls were held together with toothpicks and mayonnaise to form skaters, a snow-covered alpine lodge, and a one-horse open sleigh carrying a couple bearing the likenesses of Mr. Wiggins's boss, Nelson Lundquist, and Nelson's wife, Dot.

The Lundquists were coming over after dinner for a game of bridge. Mr. Wiggins hoped the artistic creation would help him accumulate a few brownie points.

Thomas's father was so busy making sure

he didn't jostle the precarious assembly of cheddar, Havarti, and brie that he didn't notice the presence of an additional dog in the house. Suddenly, Miss Pooch got an uncontrollable urge to race up the stairs, take a flying leap, and land right on top of the platter. She had a passion for cheese. Her movements were so swift and unpredictable even McGrowl couldn't derail her.

Before the cheese could hit the ground, McGrowl raced at supersonic speed, caught the platter, and gently deposited it on the floor. Not one cheese ball was out of place. This all occurred so quickly that Mr. Wiggins never even realized what was happening.

By the time Thomas's father brushed himself off and regained his composure, McGrowl had ushered Miss Pooch swiftly into the backyard. Spending an evening alone with the irascible little dog wasn't exactly high on McGrowl's list of things to do on a Friday night. But it had to be done.

"Nice day at school, sweetheart?" Mrs. Wiggins said as she spooned out carefully measured portions of tuna noodle surprise, one of Thomas's least favorite dinners. The only surprising thing about the dish as far as Thomas was concerned was how dry and tasteless the combination of two of his favorite foods could manage to be. This was a dish that no one could make taste good. Not even his mother.

"We had a Wilderness Weekend meeting," Thomas replied.

"That's nice," Mr. Wiggins replied distractedly. He was silently running over a few choice anecdotes with which to regale Mr. Lundquist at the bridge game.

"Pop Wheeler invited McGrowl to come

along on the trip. Isn't that great?" Thomas said enthusiastically.

His parents exchanged a flurry of anxious looks. Thomas didn't seem to notice. He was busy trying to swallow a bit of food that had been resisting all efforts to be chewed into smaller pieces when he discovered another surprising fact about tonight's dinner. It was impossible to consume without drinking massive quantities of water. Thomas raced into the kitchen to refill his glass. He felt like the raccoon in Stuart Seltzer's oral report.

"Son," Mrs. Wiggins said when he had returned, "your father has something he'd like to say to you."

Thomas looked up expectantly at Mr. Wiggins, who looked over at Mrs. Wiggins, totally confused. "I do?" he said uncertainly. Mrs. Wiggins nodded a discreet yes.

"Can you give me some kind of hint?" Mr. Wiggins asked hopefully.

"The thing we talked about this morning before breakfast? You remember," Mrs. Wiggins whispered softly. As she spoke, she turned away and covered her mouth with her napkin, pretending to wipe a speck of food from her lip. Like an ostrich, Thomas's mother believed that if she couldn't see *you,* you couldn't see her.

Mr. Wiggins stumbled forward blindly. "Thomas, your mother and I . . . um . . . well, the truth is . . . actually, we have been quite concerned . . ."

"Actually, that's not what we said at all," Mrs. Wiggins said briskly. "Thomas, we want you to know how much confidence we have in you and what a wonderful boy we think you are." She spoke in a pleasant but not altogether reassuring voice.

"Well, thanks," Thomas replied cautiously. When Mrs. Wiggins had something difficult to say, she frequently began with a compliment.

"But your father and I have been thinking." At this point Mrs. Wiggins put her napkin in her lap, sat back in her chair, and stopped eating altogether. She was about to pitch a serious curve. Thomas recognized the windup.

"You know, honey," Mrs. Wiggins began, "sometimes a person can have too much of a good thing. A little candy is good. A lot of candy can make you sick. Do you know what I'm getting at, sweetie?"

"I guess so," Thomas replied cautiously.

Mrs. Wiggins went on to explain that both she and Mr. Wiggins were concerned that Thomas was becoming too attached to McGrowl. "We'd love to see you make some new friends. And not necessarily ones with four legs and fur."

"But Mom," Thomas replied, "Lenny Winkleman and I have been hanging out a lot together. We're getting to be really close."

This was not altogether true. He and Lenny

had attempted to get together several times, but Lenny always canceled at the last minute. He had pleaded a sore throat in one case and, in another, an infected hangnail.

"One new friend doth not a summer make," Mr. Wiggins said cryptically.

"Not that we don't absolutely love Mc-Growl, sweetie," Mrs. Wiggins continued. "It's just that we'd like you to make more of an effort to reach out to other, you know . . . humans." And then she mentioned words like *self-reliance* and *personal growth.*

"I guess this means McGrowl can't come to Wilderness Weekend," Thomas said softly.

"'Fraid so, sport," Mr. Wiggins replied gently.

"We hope you understand, honey," his mother added, clearing the table. "It's really for your own good." Then she disappeared into the kitchen to get dessert.

Without any warning, Miss Pooch came

scrambling into the dining room and leaped onto the table. Before Thomas had a chance to stop her, she grabbed a huge portion of tuna noodle surprise and went racing upstairs to eat it. Bits of tuna and noodles were everywhere.

Mr. Wiggins stood up, waved his arms frantically, and yelled, "Wild animal in the house!"

As if on cue, McGrowl came screeching into the room. He had taken off after Miss Pooch in a burst of superspeed and was unable to apply the brakes in time to avoid crashing right into Mr. Wiggins. The poor man went flying into the arms of Mrs. Wiggins, who had emerged from the kitchen carrying a freshly baked blueberry pie. Three weeks later she would still be picking blueberries out of the lace curtains.

After an emergency family meeting, three things were perfectly clear. One: Miss Pooch would be allowed to stay for the weekend only if she remained outside. Two: Under no circumstances was she ever to be invited again. Three: There was no way Mr. Wiggins would recover in time to play bridge with the Lundquists.

After the family meeting, Mr. Wiggins retreated to the safety of his bathroom. He brought several issues of *This Old House* magazine and *The Wall Street Journal* with him. He wasn't planning on coming out anytime in the near future.

Poor McGrowl had to stay out in the garage with Miss Pooch. He sent a telepathic message to Thomas, letting him know that he wasn't happy about the situation.

"I'm really sorry," Thomas said as he attached Miss Pooch's leash to McGrowl's collar. "It's just for the weekend." McGrowl didn't even bother to reply.

Miss Pooch didn't put up a fuss. She was thrilled to spend the evening so close to the dog of her dreams. McGrowl, however, did not view the situation through the same rose-colored glasses. If he couldn't stand the sight of the bullwawa before tonight, being chained to her for the weekend was not likely to improve the relationship. Or so it seemed.

The Lundquists were disappointed to learn that the game had been canceled but were quite understanding when Mrs. Wiggins explained she was having a problem with her septic tank.

Thomas went upstairs to finish packing for Wilderness Weekend while his mother baked a batch of scones, assembled a meat loaf, sewed on a few more name tags, and repaired the toaster oven. Then she went upstairs to tuck Thomas in. She kissed his forehead, stationed herself at the edge of his bed, and began to speak.

"You'll probably find this hard to believe, but when I was a little girl, I loved to go camping." She smiled sweetly.

"Really?" Thomas replied. He couldn't help but smile back. It was hard to picture his perfectly neat and tidy mother wandering through the mud or pitching a tent or doing any of the millions of things campers did.

"When I was eleven, Martha Swinksy and I went on a canoe trip." As she spoke, she drew little circles on the floor with her toe. "We had so much fun. We caught a trout. I grew too fond of it to eat it, so we threw it back and had jelly beans and popcorn for dinner that night. We got so sick our mothers had to come and take us home. Two days later, I had my appendix removed. I don't think I've ever had a better time."

She stared out the window as if she could see herself and little Martha somewhere out there in the moonlit sky.

Thomas was looking at his mother in a new light. Whenever he imagined her as a child, she always looked and acted exactly as she did now, only she was shorter, and she didn't wear reading glasses.

"When you were little, did you ever get scared?" Thomas said softly. "I was just wondering." Thomas was suddenly feeling very lonely. The prospect of attending Wilderness Weekend without his best canine friend while an evil stranger was on the loose was not a happy one.

His mother brushed a stray lock of Thomas's hair off his forehead, and then she spoke. "I barely slept through the night until I was twelve years old. I was positive monsters would sneak in and take me away. I kept all the lights on, and I put a baseball bat at the foot of my bed. You should have seen the circles under my eyes."

"What happened?" Thomas asked with more than a little curiosity. In his case, the prospect of monsters — or evil strangers —

in the night was not necessarily out of the question.

"Well, finally my mother got tired of coming into my room to check on me, so she gave me a magical rock. She said her mother had given it to her and it had been in the family for generations. I have no idea if this was true. But I do know this. The minute she gave me the rock, I slept like a baby. And I was never scared of monsters again."

Mrs. Wiggins reached into the pocket of her apron and took out a small, smooth stone. She pressed it into Thomas's hand silently.

Thomas thought for a while and then looked up at his mother. "I think I'm going to have a really good time this weekend." Then he turned over and arranged his pillow so that it covered both ears and cradled his neck at just the right angle.

He thought about digging for earthworms

and making fires by rubbing two sticks to-gether. He thought about looking for nuts and berries and playing hide-and-seek in the woods. He thought about playing with Violet and Lenny and Stuart Seltzer and looking up at the stars at night.

By the time his mother tiptoed out the room and turned out the lights, Thomas was well on his way to dreamland, his magical rock clutched tightly in his hand.

Mrs. Wiggins paused in the doorway and stared lovingly at her son. She wondered, as parents frequently do, whether she had made the right decision. Perhaps she should have allowed McGrowl to go on the trip to Devil's Island after all. Somewhere in the back of her mind she had a premonition of danger. Noth-ing she could put her finger on — just the tini-est whisper of a thought. She sighed a little sigh and disappeared down the hallway.

EVERY DOG HAS HIS DAY

In the garage, McGrowl and Miss Pooch were settling down for the evening, exhausted from their busy night. McGrowl had finally managed to tire out the inexhaustible bullwawa by running with her in endless circles around the house. As he ran, he scanned the neighborhood with his powerful eyes and ears. The evil stranger and his accomplice were nowhere to be found.

Maybe I was wrong, McGrowl thought. *Maybe they've changed their minds and decided to leave us alone.* Two or three times he circled the pillow Thomas had brought outside for him, and then he lay down quietly. Miss Pooch was already snoring away on a nearby pillow.

He looked over at the dog thoughtfully. Now that she was finally asleep, he noticed she didn't really look like a man-eating fish. In fact, there was something oddly charming about the dog's tiny pink nose and the way her pointy little teeth protruded from her lower jaw.

From a tiny window on the far side of town, a pair of cold and watchful eyes stared, unnoticed, at the house. Milton Smudge put down his high-powered infrared binoculars and sighed his own particular kind of sigh, which in his case sounded more like a wheeze or a rattle.

Smudge was hiding. And looking. And waiting patiently. He tingled with anticipation. He and his accomplice would make their dreaded appearance just when the boy and the dog least expected. The chase would soon be on.

And this time, not even McGrowl would be able to spot them.

CHAPTER SIX
Into the Woods

Saturday morning passed in a blur of activity and excitement. Thomas lost his rubber boots. Mrs. Wiggins found them in the closet. Mr. Wiggins lost his car keys. Thomas found them in the garbage. Mr. Wiggins hugged Thomas, gave him a big pat on the back, and rushed off to play golf with a new client.

Finally, Mrs. Wiggins, McGrowl, and Miss Pooch said good-bye to Thomas. He raced down the street to the waiting bus, his magical rock tucked safely in his pocket. Violet was already aboard, playing a lively game of

In My Grandmother's Suitcase I Packed an Umbrella with Ralph Sidell and Sophie Morris.

Before Thomas dashed off, McGrowl managed to slip a bologna sandwich into his pocket. He imagined the boy might soon grow weary of a diet of food eaten by early settlers.

Mrs. Wiggins kept up the best face she could. But the minute Thomas was out of sight, her handkerchief emerged, her shoulders heaved, and she began to cry.

McGrowl offered her his paw and attempted to console her by making low, sympathetic growling sounds in the back of his throat, which did make her feel somewhat better. Even Miss Pooch attempted to comfort the woman by rolling over and offering up her silky belly for scratching. Mrs. Wiggins was so impressed with Miss Pooch's behavior, she took the little dog off the leash that held her tethered to McGrowl. Miss Pooch certainly seemed a lot calmer this morning.

"You're a good dog, Miss Pooch," Mrs. Wiggins said graciously.

But no sooner were the words out of her mouth than Miss Pooch jumped up and started digging away at Mrs. Wiggins's perfect front lawn. McGrowl tried to restrain her, but Miss Pooch managed to elude him. She started running across the street, barking loudly at everything she saw.

She barked at a pigeon, she barked at a car. She even barked at a garbage can. McGrowl couldn't imagine how such a big noise could come out of such a small animal.

McGrowl caught up with her as quickly as he could and carefully herded her back to the Wiggins's front yard. Mrs. Wiggins managed to slip on Miss Pooch's leash and lead her back into the garage.

"Sorry, Miss Pooch," Mrs. Wiggins said, "but until you learn to behave, we're going to have to keep you in here."

McGrowl looked over at Miss Pooch sternly. She didn't seem the slightest bit upset. She barked happily at McGrowl as if to say "I'm having a wonderful time" and proceeded to eat a cardboard box that held Mrs. Wiggins's entire collection of last year's *Martha Stewart Living* magazines. At last, McGrowl was able to wrestle the box away from her, and Mrs. Wiggins brought her prized collection into the safety of the front hall closet.

Then McGrowl helped Mrs. Wiggins do the breakfast dishes. She had grown to depend on the trusty dog in a million different ways. In fact, Mrs. Wiggins enjoyed his company more than she cared to admit.

When the last dish had been dried and put away, McGrowl swept the floor with his bushy tail and Mrs. Wiggins poured herself a big cup of coffee. Then she emptied the rest of the pot into McGrowl's shiny bowl, adding a pinch of vanilla and just the right amount of cream and sugar.

McGrowl loved Mrs. Wiggins's café au lait as much as he loved her homemade cheese Danish and chocolate streusel. As he drank, he made loud slurping sounds. The kitchen curtains fluttered madly in the breeze created by his swiftly wagging tail. Mrs. Wiggins smiled when she looked over and saw the big milk mustache that had formed over the dog's upper lip.

"What do you think, McGrowl?" she asked in a quivery voice. She was sitting down at last and taking a delicate sip of the delicious brew. "Will my boy be all right?"

McGrowl certainly hoped so, but he wasn't about to let Mrs. Wiggins know he understood every word she was saying. She reached over and scratched the back of his neck, right near his collar. McGrowl felt his ears relax. Even the knot of shoulder tension that formed whenever his boy was out of sight began to disappear.

"Look at yourself, Stacey Wiggins," she said. "Next thing you know, you'll be asking that dog his opinion about the weather."

Highs in the midfifties, McGrowl said to himself, *with ten-mile-per-hour winds and a forty percent chance of showers.* He was glad Thomas had brought along his waterproof poncho. The last thing he wanted was for his boy to return with a cold.

Meanwhile, Pop and Mamie stood on the shore of Lake Wappinger eagerly awaiting the bus. When it arrived, the excited students emerged, yelling and screaming, as they finished the last twenty choruses of "We're Here Because We're Here Because We're Here." During the bus trip, team captains had been selected and the campers had been divided into two teams: the Browns and the Greens.

"Say, where's that adorable dog?" Pop asked when he spotted Thomas and Violet but no furry yellow companion.

"My parents wouldn't let him come," Thomas replied. "I'm awfully sorry." Both Pop and Mamie seemed genuinely disappointed to find out about the Wigginses' decision.

"I even baked him his very own bone-shaped cinammon bun," Mamie said forlornly.

They certainly do love animals, Violet thought.

And then Pop and Mamie loaded everyone into canoes. Pop blew the whistle that dangled from the lanyard that encircled his doughy neck, giving the sign for the games to begin. Browns and Greens threw on life jackets and started furiously paddling the short distance across Lake Wappinger to Devil's Island. Everyone was eager to win the five points awarded to the swiftest navigators.

Stuart Seltzer, the captain of the Brown Team, yelled encouragement from his speeding canoe. Thomas and Violet paddled as quickly as they could. They were glad to be Browns. Stuart was a good leader. He had given his team a valuable pep talk on the bus. He had also taught his team members the fine art of feathering their paddles.

By twisting your paddle artfully in between strokes, you could lessen wind resistance, paddle more quickly, and tire less easily. Even so, both Violet and Thomas were quickly out of breath. They could barely join in the team chant, "Browns aren't clowns, Browns aren't clowns."

They pulled easily ahead of their nearest competitors, Sophie Morris and Lenny Winkleman, who were Greens and none too happy about it. First of all, Lewis Musser was the Green Team captain. He had won by default. Once he declared himself a candidate, everyone was afraid to nominate anyone else. Lewis knew absolutely nothing about canoeing or nature or even tent building. He had given his team no helpful hints other than to let them know that if they didn't win they'd be furnishing him with free snacks for the rest of the semester.

Second of all, Sophie and Lenny didn't get along very well. As they paddled, Sophie ordered Lenny around as if they were in the army and she was his personal sergeant. "Get busy there, soldier," she shrieked loudly. Then she started counting off strokes as if they were push-ups. "Hup, two, three, four, drop to the floor and do it some more."

She had recently watched a World War II movie on television and had discovered several new ways to boss people around. Poor Lenny had no idea what she was talking about. He was having a hard enough time coping with a splinter he had just gotten from his decaying paddle.

While the kids canoed, Pop and Mamie

jumped into a waiting motorboat and made the journey to Devil's Island in an effortless three and a half minutes.

"Let's hear it for the Brown Team," Pop cried out enthusiastically. He was already perched on a lifeguard's chair on the beach, cheering the campers as they landed on Devil's Island. The sun was shining, and the temperature was hovering at a comfortable fifty-five degrees. It was an altogether perfect day.

Finally, all thirty children arrived, happy yet exhausted from their watery journey. Pop blew his whistle for silence and declared the winner. The Browns had beaten the Greens by a full three seconds.

Thomas looked over excitedly at Violet. They were thrilled to have won the first competition of the day. Mr. Postino, the Green Team faculty adviser, waved his feather-laden cap in the air and led the cheer: "Two, four, six, eight, who do we appreciate? Brown

Team, Brown Team, yaaay!" The children all joined in, shouting and jumping up and down vigorously as Miss Thompson, the Brown Team faculty adviser, looked around furtively for snakes.

Not to be outdone, the Brown Team gave a rousing cheer of support for the losing Green Team. "We love you, Green, you're never mean, on you we're keen, yaaay!" There would be a prize at the end of the weekend for the team that demonstrated the best sportsmanship.

The Green Team hurled an even livelier cheer right back at the Brown Team: "Browns are nice, don't think twice, they're not mice, yaaay!"

Mamie called an end to the cheering and led both teams over to the campground. She was about to demonstrate proper tent-building skills. This was a sight nobody wanted to miss.

On the way, Stuart Seltzer unearthed what he took to be the cocoon of a rare and beautiful luna moth and proudly showed it off to

tiful luna moth and proudly showed it off to everyone. Pop ran over to take a look and discovered that Stuart's cocoon was actually a chunk of petrified candy bar from last year's trip to the island.

"We're giving your team one point anyway, young man. After all, you *could* have found a cocoon," Pop said. He went on to explain that cocoons, snails, and earthworms were worth between one to three points each, depending on their size and condition.

Chipmunks and gophers, which thrived on the little island, were worth five to seven points each, but you weren't allowed to touch them. You needed to have your sighting confirmed by at least two other team members, all of whom had taken a solemn oath to tell the truth.

On Wilderness Weekend no opportunity was missed to turn the simplest activity into a competition. The team to drink the most water would be awarded six points. The first person to spot a falling star would be given four points. The camper who flossed the longest would receive two points and extra dessert.

"To begin with, children," Mamie said in a voice filled with confidence and authority, "we must first locate a flat piece of land upon which to place the tent. One cannot be too careful when choosing a correct site. The three most important rules of good tent building are," she paused dramatically, "location, location, location."

Tent building with Mamie continued for a while without a hitch. The crowd of fifth-graders that had assembled to watch was noticeably let down. They had come expecting to witness one of Mamie's hilarious mistakes. They wouldn't be disappointed for long.

CHAPTER SEVEN
Winners and Losers

"When you have confirmed your selection," Mamie said, "prepare the land for the arrival of the tent by hopping up and down with a firm but graceful step." She began leaping about the area. The crowd leaned forward hopefully.

"This will provide the camper with tremendous aerobic benefits, as well as destroy any stray bits of annoying vegetation or unwanted insect life." Huffing and puffing mightily, Mamie continued heaving all of her two hundred and twenty pounds as high into the air as she could, then crashing back to earth with a tremendous force that made the ground shake. "The harder, the better, kids. Don't be afraid to pound, pound, pound," she exhorted.

Unfortunately, the area upon which she was leaping was home to a large family of gophers. They had recently carved out an elaborate underground network of long, winding tunnels. In other words, the earth upon which Mamie was stomping was about as solid as a pile of Swiss cheese.

Already the gopher family had grabbed a few belongings and had raced to resettle in a safer, quieter territory.

"Heeeelp!" Mamie screamed as the ground beneath her suddenly gave way and she disappeared as tidily as if she had been vaporized. At first, the children feared for her safety, but Mamie popped up from the hole in the ground a moment later. She was covered with dirt and grass.

Clearly unharmed, she exclaimed happily, "Campers, never do what I do. Come to think of it, never do what I *say*, either." Thomas smiled at Violet, who flashed back an enthusiastic grin. So far, Wilderness Weekend was even more fun than they had thought it would be.

And then Thomas thought about Gosling Fletch and wondered whether McGrowl had encountered him again. Violet noticed the worried look cross his face. "Are you okay?" she wondered.

Thomas telepathically beamed his concern to McGrowl, who instantly beamed back a reply. He told Thomas he was fine, and Gosling was nowhere to be seen.

"I'm great," Thomas replied happily to Violet.

Then Thomas, Violet, and the other campers participated in an exciting afternoon of wilderness survival activities. Browns and Greens competed in the "Boil, Water, Boil" competition. Campers lit a campfire by rubbing two sticks together. Then water in an old tin cup was brought to a furious boil while campers shouted, "Boil, water, boil!" This event alone took up the better part of two hours. Eventually, the Green Team won for shouting the loudest, but everyone got a sore throat.

Next, the Browns and the Greens had a jumping and hopping contest across a particularly rocky part of the island. Stuart Seltzer got a bloody nose when he slipped on a mossy patch, but everyone else survived without so much as a scratch.

Meanwhile, McGrowl did his best to keep Miss Pooch out of trouble. He decided to take her on a tour of the neighborhood. Mr. Wiggins had returned from his golf match. McGrowl realized that keeping Miss Pooch in sight of the recently traumatized man was a recipe for disaster.

The garbage dump was first on McGrowl's list of local sights to see. Not only did it give off an abundance of exotic smells, the chances of finding a discarded bone from Mr. McCarthy's grocery store were good. Miss Pooch, however, had other plans. She decided it would be a perfect day to chase cats. She tried to break away from McGrowl at every opportunity and look for her favorite prey.

By the time they were halfway to the dump, McGrowl was exhausted. Trying to keep Miss Pooch out of trouble was a handful even for a bionic dog. When she wasn't trying to escape, she was jumping all over McGrowl and nipping at him with her sharp little teeth. McGrowl barked menacingly. Miss Pooch took this as a sign that he wanted to play. She leaped onto his back, yipping happily. McGrowl's patience was wearing thin.

Just as they were about to arrive at the dump, McGrowl spotted the cat — his enemy — across the street. He hadn't seen her for months. She had been out of town with her owners. McGrowl hated that cat. She tormented him whenever she could, and had so far eluded McGrowl's many attempts to capture her.

As McGrowl debated leaving Miss Pooch to her own devices and making a dash for the cat, Miss Pooch took matters into her own paws and started chasing the cat herself. McGrowl followed close behind. The cat spotted her pursuers, wagged her tail irritatingly, and scampered away.

Miss Pooch darted across the street and nearly got run over by Mr. McCarthy's grocery truck. The truck swerved to avoid Miss Pooch and ended up on Stella Hoenig's front lawn, flattening several rosebushes instead of the bullwawa.

Mrs. Hoenig poked her head out her living room window. "I don't believe we ordered home delivery today, Mr. McCarthy, but thanks anyway," she said, and disappeared back into her house.

Poor Mr. McCarthy. As he maneuvered his truck back onto the street, Officer Nelson came by and wrote him a ticket for driving on the grass.

Meanwhile, the cat dashed down the nearest alley and headed for the safety of the large sycamore tree in front of her house. If she could make it to the tree, she could climb to its upper branches, jump onto the roof, and climb into the house through an upstairs window. She knew McGrowl would never enter her house. On their many chases, he had never followed her inside.

What the cat hadn't counted on was the

fact that Miss Pooch had no fear whatsoever of going where she wasn't supposed to go.

As the cat shimmied up the tree, McGrowl chased after her. His powerful paws propelled him steadily up the trunk. Miss Pooch jumped onto his back and clung to his collar with all her might. She barked at McGrowl to climb faster. She was having the time of her life.

The poor cat scrambled madly to the tip of the tallest branch, jumped onto the roof, climbed in through the window, and breathed a sigh of relief.

McGrowl stopped abruptly, but Miss Pooch took a flying leap off his back and sailed through the window after the cat. McGrowl shook his head in amazement.

Miss Pooch had the cat cornered in an up-stairs bedroom and was barking loudly. The cat arched her back. She bared her claws and hissed and screamed. Fur was about to fly. McGrowl barked supportively.

The cat's owner ran into the room to see what all the fuss was about. She took her precious cat in her arms and started chasing after Miss Pooch with the broom she happened to be carrying. "Get out of here, you nasty thing!" she yelled at the bullwawa. Miss Pooch ran out the window and jumped onto McGrowl's back. He carried her quickly down the tree and across the lawn.

In a minute, the two dogs were trotting down the sidewalk together, continuing toward their original destination — the garbage dump. McGrowl looked over at Miss Pooch with a mixture of concern and admiration. She certainly was a handful. But he had to admit she was also a lot of fun.

● ●

An army of tired and dirty campers trooped into the dining tent and were extremely relieved to discover that supper consisted of burgers, hot dogs, and mountains of potato chips — not nuts and berries. Dessert was s'mores. The Green Team ate thirteen more of the toasted chocolate-and-marshmallow treats than the Brown Team. Both teams felt equally nauseous.

By the time a prerecorded bugle sounded taps over the speakers, everyone was already asleep and looking forward to another full day of events. The Greens were ahead by six points. But the Browns weren't about to go down without a struggle.

Thomas tossed and turned in his sleeping bag. He was dreaming about Gosling Fletch and his accomplice. They were chasing him, and he was trying to send McGrowl a message, but McGrowl was having trouble receiving it.

And then Thomas awoke with a start and realized it was just a dream. He looked around at the other campers. They were sleeping peacefully. *Go back to sleep,* he told himself. And he did. This time he dreamed of pinecones, gophers, and a beautiful sunset over Lake Wappinger.

At the Wiggins household as well, lights were out and sleeping caps were firmly in place. Mrs. Wiggins looked over at Mr. Wiggins. He was sound asleep, fully dressed, in case of a sudden dog attack. He didn't have anything to worry about.

McGrowl and Miss Pooch were sleeping peacefully in the garage, atop the same fluffy pillow. Miss Pooch had become frightened in the night, and McGrowl had graciously made room for the little dog beside him on his ample cushion.

Bullwawas, he was beginning to think, *aren't so bad after all.* Miss Pooch nestled against his fuzzy flank and was snoring in less than a minute. McGrowl was snoring in less than two.

CHAPTER EIGHT
Ghosts

Sunday morning began promisingly. Timothy Hunsinger won three points for the Green Team by eating more bacon than anyone thought was humanly possible. Lenny Winkleman collected two points for cleanest fingernails. Violet got four points for best table manners.

Sophie Morris protested bitterly. She couldn't understand how she had managed to lose after memorizing every single word of *Miss Manners' Guide to Proper Dining.* Unfortunately, she had skipped the entire chapter on proper use of the napkin and had used the edge of the tablecloth to wipe a ketchup dollop from her blouse.

The highlight of the afternoon was fishing for the delicious perch that were rumored to inhabit Lake Wappinger. Thirty campers sat on the dock with thirty fishing poles baited with thirty worms and waited eagerly. Not one single fish, perch or otherwise, was even spotted.

The Brown Team began to chant, "Catch a blue, catch a blue, don't come back with a torn old shoe." The Green Team retorted with a snappy "We love fish, we love fish, in the lake or on a dish."

And then Lenny Winkleman's rod starting straining as a great big walleyed pike took his bait and started swimming to the middle of the lake with it. Lenny put up a noble fight as all the campers joined in a cheer, "We love you, Lenny, more than a penny, catch that fish, or we won't have any."

EVERY DOG HAS HIS DAY

Lenny pulled with all his might and reeled in the fish as it wriggled and jumped and tried to get away. Even Miss Thompson joined in the excitement. She stood right next to Lenny and yelled in his ear, "Go, Lenny, go, don't step on your toe."

After several minutes of intense struggling, Lenny was about to land his catch. No one could believe their eyes. Lenny Winkleman never succeeded at anything. Even though he was the captain of Lenny's team, Lewis Musser was green with envy.

The flopping fish struggled to get away as Lenny lifted it from the water and did something so startling the others campers fell silent and stared in disbelief. Lenny carefully disengaged the hook from the wriggling fish's mouth and tossed it in the water.

In a flash, the fish was racing back to the middle of the lake, grateful and happy for its freedom. A loud chorus of groans arose from the crowd, and Lewis Musser started yelling at Lenny. "You're nothing but a stupid baby, Finkleman. I don't even want you on my team."

Lenny looked like he was about to burst into tears. He didn't mean to lose points for his team. He just couldn't bear the idea of hurting that beautiful, proud fish.

Thomas didn't happen to think letting the fish go was such a bad idea. He came forward and stationed himself between Lewis and Lenny.

"Take it back," Thomas said. He spoke quietly but firmly.

"What are you saying, dork-face?" Lewis couldn't believe his ears. Thomas Wiggins, the quietest boy in the class, was standing up to him. "Say it again — I dare you."

Thomas hadn't even meant to stand up to the bully. He just couldn't stand to watch Lenny being picked on. "You don't have to be mean to Lenny. It's not nice," Thomas said.

As he spoke, his face flushed and his legs started shaking. Lewis could flatten him in a second if he wanted to. Violet looked over at Thomas proudly, glad to be his friend.

Every head on the island turned to Lewis to see what he was going to do. Pop and Mamie watched apprehensively, prepared to step in and break up a fight. Miss Thompson chewed nervously on a feather.

"You better watch your step, Wiggins," Lewis said threateningly. He puffed himself up and poked Thomas in the chest. "You've got one more chance, then I'm letting you have it." And he turned and walked away.

Thomas had just learned a valuable lesson: Standing up to bullies wasn't always danger-ous. Sometimes their bark was a whole lot worse than their bite. It was a lesson he would never forget.

And then everyone rushed to change for dinner. There would be a campfire tonight.

Violet was planning to tell one of her famous ghost stories. She had been practicing in front of the mirror for days. Even Thomas, who had heard the story a number of times, confessed to getting goose bumps at the very thought of it.

• •

Meanwhile, back at 27 Walnut Grove Avenue, Mrs. Wiggins had just finished the dinner dishes. She was putting together a five-thousand-piece jigsaw puzzle she had received for Mother's Day. It depicted the National Tupperware Museum.

Mr. Wiggins was at the craft store buying lacquer to preserve the puzzle when it was finished. In the last rays of the setting sun, McGrowl was in the backyard teaching Miss Pooch how to throw a Frisbee. The little dog had quick reflexes and strong hind legs. She was an excellent student.

All of a sudden, the unmistakable odor of

formaldehyde drifted into the yard. McGrowl rushed Miss Pooch safely back into the garage, where she waited patiently for the next exciting event to begin. A weekend with Mc-Growl was full of more fun than she had had in her entire young life.

McGrowl scratched at the back door and barked to be let in. Before Mrs. Wiggins had a chance to open the back door, the front door-bell rang.

As Mrs. Wiggins hurried to answer the door, McGrowl raced to the front of the house, barking loudly. The bell rang again. Who could that be, she wondered. She opened the door and stared at a glowering Gosling Fletch and the short, round woman who accompanied him. They stared right back at her. The man looked extremely unhappy.

"Madam," Mr. Fletch began, "would you kindly remove your dog's teeth from my left foot?" Mrs. Wiggins looked down, astonished.

McGrowl did indeed appear to be chewing on one of the man's enormous loafers.

Fortunately, Gosling Fletch had the peculiar habit of wearing shoes several sizes larger than his actual foot. McGrowl's teeth had damaged a perfectly good pair of shoes, size fifteen, but left the actual toes of the teacher unharmed.

"Bad dog," Mrs. Wiggins said — the two most dreaded words in all of McGrowl's vocabulary. He wanted to be a good dog more than anything in the world. He immediately removed his mouth from the shoe.

"If you would be so kind as to restrain your wild animal, my wife and I would like to have a word with you concerning your son," said Gosling Fletch. "I am a teacher at the Stevenson School." Mrs. Wiggins let him and the odd little woman into the house. The Fletches were returning from a neighborhood dinner party celebrating Albert Einstein's contributions to science, and Mr. Fletch had decided to pay a call on the Wigginses.

McGrowl couldn't take his eyes off Mrs. Fletch's enormous false nose. Nearly as wide as it was long, it dominated her tiny face. It appeared to be made of plastic or rubber. *If only I could take a quick peek beneath it,* McGrowl thought, *perhaps I could determine the woman's true identity.*

The dog leaped up suddenly, pretending to lick Mrs. Fletch's face in an outpouring of spontaneous affection. He grasped her nose firmly in his teeth and attempted to remove it with lightning-quick speed. Tug as he might, he could not loosen the nose from the woman's face. There was a good reason for that. It was permanently attached to the woman's face, and was, in fact, her actual nose. He quickly released his grip and slinked off in shame.

Mr. and Mrs. Fletch followed Mrs. Wiggins into the kitchen and sat at the table while

Thomas's mother put on a pot of coffee and warmed up one of her famous strawberry walnut dessert loaves. McGrowl stationed himself in the kitchen doorway. The Fletches seated themselves as far away from McGrowl as possible.

Why, McGrowl wondered, *is Mrs. Wiggins treating the evil stranger and his dreaded accomplice as if they are honored guests at a tea party?*

It was all McGrowl could do to restrain himself from tying up the visitors and carrying them off to the police. He didn't take his eyes off either one of them for a second. His heart was racing. What were they up to? The suspense was almost too much for McGrowl to bear.

• •

"The clock struck twelve. The footsteps grew louder. An eerie light began to fill the room. The footsteps continued. Closer and closer they came." Violet's voice was low and raspy. She leaned forward. Nobody dared to move.

The campfire was all glowing embers and crackling pinecones. A bunch of tired, over-stuffed campers were huddled around it, hanging on her every word.

Violet's tale of the haunted mansion was filled with eerie spirits, a piano that played it-self, and a bloody severed hand. It had taken on a chilling quality that was proving chal-lenging for some of the faint of heart.

She continued, "Something was walking down the hallway. You could hear its labored breathing. It seemed to be dragging chains. *Clank, clank, clank.* Closer and closer it came. Suddenly, a scream like a roaring freight train pierced the silence of the room . . . *heeeeeelp!*" Violet let loose with her most terrifying scream.

"Stop!" Sophie Morris cried out loudly. She was already hiding her face under her jacket and covering both ears with her hands.

"I want to go home," Lenny Winkleman moaned, echoing the sentiments of a number of the other campers. Even Lewis Musser was looking a little shaky.

Violet hadn't even gotten to the best part. In a moment, Thomas would sneak up behind an unsuspecting listener and drop leaves on his or her head.

Pop Wheeler stood to address the crowd. "Intermission," he called out. The kids breathed a collective sigh of relief. Thomas sat down immediately and hid his leaves.

"Tell us, Esther Mueller," Pop went on, "you see a ghost in your tent tonight, and you're all alone. There's no teacher around. Quick. What d'ya do?" He added a measure of drama to the moment by taking out his flashlight and shining it right into the terrified girl's eyes. Twenty-nine anxious young faces leaned forward, waiting to hear the answer.

Little Esther carefully considered the question. She was a solid B+ student and prided herself on her thoughtful answers. "I'm not a hundred percent sure. But this is what I think." She bit her lower lip, closed her eyes, and concentrated with all her might.

"I think if you see a ghost in your tent and you're all alone . . . you should throw pepper at his nose . . . and he'll sneeze so hard his sheet will fall off . . . and he'll have to go back to the netherworld from whence he came. I believe I read that once in a book about the paranormal." Esther was especially proud of herself for her use of the word *whence.*

"That's a very good answer, Esther," Pop said. Esther smiled proudly. Already Lenny Winkleman was wondering why his mother hadn't packed any pepper in his overnight case. "But not a correct answer." Esther's smile vanished.

"What you should do if you see a ghost in your tent is have your eyes examined because — why, campers?" Pop asked.

"There's no such thing as ghosts," several children shouted back happily.

"I can't hear you," Pop said, and put his hands up to his ears as if to capture the faint sound of the crowd.

This time every camper screamed the answer back. "THERE'S NO SUCH THING AS GHOSTS!"

"I still can't hear you," Pop called out, and then quickly added, "two points for the team that yells the loudest." The challenge resulted in a symphony of screeching and hollering. Birds in distant trees awoke and began chirping, thinking it was morning. The little family of gophers looked up from their new home and shook their heads. They decided it was time to relocate yet again and moved even deeper into the forest.

Lenny wasn't convinced. He decided that he would never go camping again without a large supply of pepper.

Pop awarded the storytelling prize to the Browns, as long as Violet promised never to tell the rest of her tale. He declared the yelling contest a draw and awarded each team two points for effort. Then everyone went back to their tents to begin the flossing contest and get ready for bed.

As the entire group lay in their sleeping bags and joined in several rousing choruses of "Michael, Row Your Boat Ashore," Miss Thompson examined her bedroll for the umpteenth time. She was convinced that a reptile might be lurking somewhere inside. She finally decided to sleep on top of the covers, avoiding altogether the possibility of finding a snake in her bed.

One by one, the lanterns in the tents were extinguished, and exhausted campers fell asleep dreaming of canoes, marshmallows, and ghosts with pepper in their noses. Outside, stars twinkled brightly in the cool night air, and an occasional owl hooted mournfully in the distance. Thomas turned over in his sleeping bag and thought about what a wonderful time he was having.

CHAPTER NINE
Don't Look Now

"And then," Gosling Fletch said, gesturing to the quiet woman who sat adoringly across from him, "my wife spilled the formaldehyde, and I ran out to get some paper towels." Henrietta Fletch nodded guiltily. Mrs. Wiggins passed out more strawberry walnut dessert loaf and tried not to stare at the woman's nose.

The teacher continued. "We had to clean the entire classroom from top to bottom, and we still haven't gotten rid of that awful odor. Whatever you do," Mr. Fletch said urgently, "avoid spilling large quantities of formalde-hyde, Mrs. Wiggins. The stench is overpow-ering."

Mrs. Wiggins nodded sympathetically. "I can only imagine." She was painfully aware that both the man and his wife still smelled dreadful.

"I was literally drenched in the stuff. My shoes had to be discarded and new ones purchased immediately." Mr. Fletch looked sadly down at his recently purchased, now chewed-up shoe. McGrowl listened with great interest. *So that explains the formalde-hyde odor,* he thought to himself. The dog looked away, confused. He had been certain that Gosling Fletch was Milton Smudge in disguise. Had he and Thomas been mis-taken?

"How perfectly fascinating," Mrs. Wiggins said. She did her best to appear interested as she cut a few more slices of the dessert loaf.

"Care for another nose, Mrs. Fletch?" Mrs. Wiggins quickly turned a bright shade of red. "I mean . . . another slice?"

Both Fletches took more. Then, with a sudden flourish, the teacher reached into his pocket and removed the crumpled brown paper bag Thomas and McGrowl had taken from the trash basket in the biology lab.

McGrowl watched as Fletch reached into the bag and pulled out a laminated piece of paper about the size of a credit card. The dog strained to get a better look at the card, which appeared to indicate membership in a club of some kind. It was decorated with drawings of molecules and atoms.

"I trust you'll see that Thomas gets this back. I've been attempting to return it to your son since I discovered it in my classroom on Friday afternoon. Apparently, he dropped it while riffling through my discarded lunch sack," Mr. Fletch said as he handed the card

117

over to Mrs. Wiggins with great disdain. Mc-Growl's eyes widened. *So that's why Mr. Fletch was pursuing Thomas so eagerly!* he thought.

"Now, what he and that creature," he cast a wary glance over at McGrowl, who was doing his best to appear as docile as possible, "were doing in my classroom during recess was and continues to be a mystery to me." Fletch paused ominously and leaned forward in his chair. "Does your son particularly enjoy the sciences, Mrs. Wiggins?"

"Why, yes, as a matter of fact, he does. And this," she held the card up, "means a lot to him. He'll be so grateful, Mr. and Mrs. Fletch. He treasures his membership in Junior Scientists of America. Where did you say he dropped it?"

"In my classroom, Mrs. Wiggins," Mr. Fletch said through a mouthful of strawberries and walnuts. "Even though he is not yet old enough to enroll in my class, perhaps as a budding young scientist he was drawn to the room. Many children are."

Fletch uncurled his long, snakelike body from the chair upon which he had been sloping and extended himself to his fullest height. His head nearly touched the ceiling. "Now, if you'll excuse us, we'll be going." He extended a gloved hand and bowed stiffly.

Shy Mrs. Fletch, who until this moment had not uttered a single word, suddenly spoke in a soft, mouselike voice. "Would you ever consider giving us the recipe for that brilliant strawberry walnut dessert loaf? We love to cook. We could share our recipe for authentic Chinese fortune cookies with you in exchange."

McGrowl listened with amazement as Mrs. Fletch went on to list what turned out to be precisely the same ingredients that comprised Mrs. Wiggins's cookies. Evidently, in their quest for the perfect exotic dessert, the two women had stumbled upon identical Chinese recipes.

"What a small, small world," Mrs. Wiggins exclaimed.

"Tiny, you could almost say," Mrs. Fletch concurred wistfully. "Miniscule, even."

"Of microscopic proportion," Gosling Fletch said, ever the science teacher.

As the Fletches left, clutching the handwritten recipe for Wiggins's Walnut Wonder, Mc-Growl felt more and more certain that he and Thomas had, indeed, made a terrible mistake.

At no time did either of the Fletches attempt to do him any harm. And the teacher did have a perfectly reasonable excuse for his strong odor and his strange behavior — he was following Thomas because he wanted to return the boy's Junior Scientists of America membership card.

EVERY DOG HAS HIS DAY

If the evil stranger isn't pretending to be Gosling Fletch, McGrowl thought, *then whose identity has he stolen this time?* He began to wish he weren't separated from Thomas by ten miles and a large body of water. For all he knew, the real evil stranger was right there on the island with Thomas, waiting to make his move.

McGrowl shuddered to think of it. Perhaps Milton Smudge had returned in the guise of Miss Thompson. Or even one of the students. Lenny Winkleman did seem to be awfully big for his age. Was Smudge clever enough to disguise himself as little Sophie Morris?

One thing was certain. With the evil stranger, anything was possible.

●●●●●●●●●●●●●●●●●●●●●●●●●●●●●●●

By now the four other campers in Thomas's tent were snoring loudly. Thomas tried counting snores. Instead of putting him to sleep, the noise only reminded him that he was awake. He tossed and turned. He thought about tomorrow's competition. He thought about s'mores. He thought about Gosling Fletch.

Thomas sat up suddenly and concentrated on the sound that was filling his head. It was McGrowl. The dog was trying to tell him something, but he was having trouble understanding the message. *Slow down,* Thomas thought, *you're going too fast.*

And then Thomas received the message. It wasn't a comforting one. The knowledge that Gosling Fletch was not Milton Smudge came floating uneasily into his brain. The thought was accompanied by a gentle reminder from McGrowl warning Thomas to keep an eye out for strange behavior on the part of his companions on the island.

McGrowl didn't want to panic Thomas, but

with Mr. Fletch no longer a prime suspect, the evil stranger could be disguised as anybody. He could be in the tent with Thomas at this very moment. Thomas promised McGrowl he would be careful. His mind was racing.

Thomas pulled his jacket on over his pajamas, stepped into his shoes, and slipped quietly outside. The air was cold, and the dampness that rose from the ground sent a chill through his body. Thomas shivered, drew his collar up over his ears, and put his hands into his pockets.

He looked up. There wasn't a cloud in the sky. Thomas loved looking at the stars. It reminded him of how tiny Earth was and how even tinier Cedar Springs was and how utterly tiny Thomas himself was. *Everything in perspective,* he reminded himself.

Even Milton Smudge didn't seem quite so important when you considered the size of the universe. He watched as a shooting star streaked across the sky. *How beautiful,* he thought. He didn't even care if he got any points for it.

"What are you doing up?" Violet whispered, interrupting his reverie.

"You could give a person a heart attack," Thomas said as he whirled around. He could feel the adrenaline pulsing through his veins.

"Sorry. Couldn't sleep," Violet whispered. She, too, had begun to shiver. "I thought I saw a ghost."

"Serves you right," Thomas said good-naturedly.

"So, what're you doing up?" Violet said, trying to stop her teeth from chattering.

"I couldn't sleep, either," Thomas replied. He started walking in the direction of the dining tent. "Maybe there's hot chocolate somewhere."

As they walked, they heard something that

sounded like heavy breathing coming from the other side of the tent.

"What was that?" Violet asked nervously.

Thomas and Violet held their breath and listened with all their might. "It's nothing," Thomas replied with as much certainty as he could muster.

Somewhere in the distance, a twig snapped. Thomas felt the hair on the back of his neck stand on end. "Gophers probably. They're everywhere," he said unconvincingly.

"Yeah. Sure. Gophers," Violet said, unconvinced. She grabbed Thomas's hand. Together, they ventured forward tentatively. Then it appeared. It rose from behind a nearby bush.

Pale and shadowy, the white-shrouded figure hovered in the moonlight. Its shapeless, billowing form fluttered in the gentle breeze that blew in from the lake. "Got any pepper?" Violet asked softly.

Don't let your imagination run away with you, Thomas thought as he rubbed his eyes and prayed for it to go away. It didn't.

Wake up, wake up, Violet said to herself. She pinched her arm. She wasn't dreaming. Something was out there.

CHAPTER TEN
Catch Me If You Can

Violet was holding on to Thomas's hand so tightly that his fingers had fallen asleep. He wriggled them back and forth until they tingled with needles and pins.

The mysterious white figure darted this way and that. It seemed to be having trouble making up its mind where it wanted to go. Suddenly, it streaked toward a little path that led to the overgrown section of woods near Harmony Hill. Pop Wheeler had warned the campers never to go there.

Violet fished a coin out of her pocket. "Heads, we go back to bed; tails, we follow the you-know-what." Violet couldn't bring herself to say "ghost."

Thomas didn't reply. He was already off like a shot in the direction of the you-know-what. Violet had to run as fast as she could to keep up with him. A blanket of fallen pine needles crunched under their feet. "C'mon, it's getting away," Thomas whispered intensely.

A cloud appeared and drifted lazily across the moon, plunging the children into darkness. Thomas shivered again. But this time it wasn't from the cold.

● ●

Thomas was in danger. McGrowl could sense it as clearly as if the boy were in the room with him. His eyes snapped open, and he looked around the darkened garage. Miss Pooch was sleeping peacefully on the pillow beside him. She stirred as McGrowl arose and paced anxiously back and forth. His nails made a clicking sound on the concrete floor.

The dog sent Thomas an urgent message. *Don't move, I'll be right there to get you.*

I'm perfectly fine, Thomas told him. *I don't need help.* McGrowl sent back a message saying he didn't believe Thomas.

Thomas replied firmly, *It's true. I'm not in any danger. I'm just chasing a ghost.*

McGrowl thought ghost chasing sounded dangerous.

Thomas replied without hesitating. *It's not scary dangerous. It's exciting dangerous.*

McGrowl still wasn't convinced. Thomas sent a final message. *There are some things I need to do for myself, McGrowl.*

Thomas's message was filled with a clear and unwavering resolve. He was certain that his parents would have been proud of his independence from McGrowl.

Unconvinced that Thomas was, indeed,

perfectly fine, McGrowl considered leaving immediately. Would Thomas be angry with him? He continued pacing, anxiously debating what to do. He wanted to be a good dog. But even more than that, he wanted Thomas to be safe.

In a minute, Mrs. Wiggins's sleepy head was poking though the garage door. She wore enormous curlers covered with a kerchief decorated with scenes of Niagara Falls. She had been having trouble sleeping, too, and decided to check in on McGrowl and Miss Pooch.

"Want to come inside and get something to eat?" she ventured. The dog was so grateful he nearly jumped up and kissed her. Food always had a calming influence on McGrowl.

• •

The mysterious white figure floated silently away. Violet caught up with Thomas. Together they tiptoed forward as quickly and as quietly as they could, terrified the ghost would hear them. They paid no attention to the branches that tore at their clothing and the wind that whipped at their faces. The temperature was dropping, and ominous rain clouds began to spread across the sky until not a star could be seen.

And still the children kept moving.

All of a sudden, the shadowy figure doubled back along the path. It seemed to be looking for something. It turned this way and that, making a series of jerky movements. Something caught its eye and it froze. It seemed to be looking directly at them.

"Duck," Thomas whispered. Both he and Violet dropped to the ground and did their best to hide behind a bush. Violet hoped it wouldn't be filled with poison ivy. "I think it sees us," Thomas said. Their hearts were pounding.

Both children lay perfectly still, not daring to move. The apparition, apparently satisfied it

wasn't being followed, floated smoothly on-
ward and disappeared down a bend in the
path. The second it was out of sight, the children took off after it again.

"What happens if we catch up with it?"
Violet asked anxiously.

Thomas decided not to answer the question. All he knew was he had to keep on moving. Despite Pop Wheeler's belief that ghosts
didn't really exist, he wasn't about to pass up
an opportunity to find out for himself. He ran
as fast as his legs would carry him. He was
absolutely terrified and having the time of his
life.

The little path twisted and turned. A flash of
lightning was followed by a distant clap of
thunder. The faint outline of the ghost could
be seen in the distance. A light rain started
to fall. Violet stopped to catch her breath.
Thomas stopped as well. He took in deep
gulps of the cold night air.

"We're running uphill," he said in between gasps. "That's why it's so hard to breathe. Look," he said, pointing ahead with a shaking finger.

Through the murky darkness ahead they could make out a towering spire of jagged rock, jutting majestically upward hundreds of feet into the air. Its peak was obscured by dark, threatening clouds. "That's Harmony Hill," Violet said, her voice shaking. "We're not supposed to be here."

"It sure doesn't look very harmonious," Thomas replied.

A bolt of lightning hurtled across the sky directly above them, followed by a crash of thunder so loud both Thomas and Violet had to cover their ears.

"Forget about the ghost, we gotta get back to our tents. We could get in big trouble," Violet said urgently.

"We could also get struck by lightning,"

Thomas said. They proceeded to run until they could run no longer and then collapsed, panting, on a fallen log.

All at once, a looming figure came crashing through the underbrush. It tripped over the log on which they were resting and landed right on top of Thomas and Violet. Violet stifled the scream that was rising in her throat. Was it the ghost?

As it fell, it called out in a familiar and un-ghostlike voice, "What in the Sam Hill is going on here?"

It was Pop Wheeler! Thomas had never been so happy to see anyone in his entire life. Pop picked himself up and wiped the mud from his pants. Then he looked Violet right in the eyes and exclaimed, "What happened to you, Mamie? You got small." He laughed his loud, reassuring laugh, raised his umbrella, and gently shielded the children from the sheets of rain that were falling. "Shouldn't you kids be sound asleep in your tents like everybody else?"

"We were out chasing a ghost," Violet said.

"Or at least something that looked like a ghost," Thomas explained.

"Was the ghost about this high," Pop raised his hand to Thomas's height, "and was it wearing a white sheet?"

"Yes!" Thomas exclaimed. "Did you see it?"

"See it?" Pop chuckled. "I'm married to it!" And in a twinkling, Mamie came rushing over. She was making a futile attempt to avoid the downpour by holding a big white sheet over her head. Thomas and Violet gave each other a knowing look.

Their ghost had been nothing more than Mamie in a white sheet. They were simultaneously relieved and disappointed.

While everyone huddled under Pop's umbrella, he explained that he and Mamie had been out picking a little-known form of blueberry called *Luna fructosa.* "Tastiest little fella you ever saw," Pop enthused. "Only grows near Harmony Hill. Loves that rocky soil."

"And you can only pick them in the dead of night," Mamie complained. "Well, I got lost, and then it started to rain. Guess we won't be having *Luna fructosa* pancakes for breakfast tomorrow morning, kids. Darn," Mamie said sadly.

"That's okay, honey, you always burn them, anyway," Pop joked.

"That's true," Mamie said cheerfully.

"Say, kids," Pop said. "It looks like the rain is letting up. Why don't you join us on a midnight *Luna fructosa* berry-picking excursion? We could certainly use the help."

"Or at least I could," Mamie added. Thomas and Violet happily agreed, and they all headed for the slopes of Harmony Hill.

"Keep your eyes open for poison ivy," Pop warned.

Suddenly, Miss Thompson came stumbling

through the bushes, screaming, "Pop and Mamie, Pop and Mamie!" Pop tried to calm the shaking woman. She was covered with twigs and leaves, and her fuzzy pink bunny slippers were torn and muddy.

Then the agitated teacher threw her arms around Mamie's comforting neck and refused to let go. Clearly, Miss Thompson had reached the end of her already heavily frayed rope.

Lewis Musser had snuck into Miss Thompson's tent earlier in the evening and slipped a rubber snake into her shoe, unnoticed. Poor Miss Thompson got up to go to the bathroom several hours later, felt it with her toes, and ran screaming into the night.

"I didn't know what to do," Miss Thompson said, panting heavily. "I thought I'd never find you. I ran and I ran."

Both Pop and Mamie did everything they could to get Miss Thompson to go back to her tent so they could resume their berry picking.

"If only as an example to the little children," Pop begged, "conquer your fear. You can do it, Miss Thompson. I know you can."

"Let me put it this way," Miss Thompson said through clenched teeth. She was holding on to Mamie's arm tightly. "You couldn't pry me loose with a ten-foot pole."

"Guess it's back to bed for all of us," Pop said reluctantly, and they all started trudging back to their tents. Miss Thompson clung to Mamie. "Say, button up those jackets, kids," Pop warned. "Don't want you to get sick. We've got a big day tomorrow."

As if on cue, Thomas and Violet sneezed identical sneezes. Thomas reached into his jacket pocket and pulled out a handful of paper tissues. He smiled. His name tag was carefully sewn onto each and every one.

Everybody said good night and returned to their tents. Miss Thompson begged Mamie to sit by the side of her sleeping bag until she fell asleep, but Pop was able to persuade her she could handle it by herself. Miss Thompson did, however, make both Pop and Mamie search her tent thoroughly before she was willing to go in.

"Pop's really nice," Thomas said as he dropped Violet off at her tent.

"I guess so." She didn't sound convinced. "But I think there's something fishy going on here."

"What do you mean?" Thomas asked.

"Well, first of all, we followed Mamie for a long time, and she didn't even try to find a berry," said Violet.

"Maybe she just didn't see any," Thomas said.

"Maybe," Violet replied. "But I've never even heard of *Luna fructosa* berries. I think Pop and Mamie made them up."

"Why would anybody lie about a berry?" Thomas asked.

"Well, maybe they didn't want us to know what they were really doing up there. Something just doesn't feel right." Violet could be very stubborn when she wanted to be. "And I didn't see any poison ivy, either. I thought Harmony Hill was supposed to be covered with the stuff."

"I hate to say it," Thomas chided, "but your imagination seems to be working overtime." Thomas's mother frequently accused him of the very same thing.

"Maybe," Violet said as she ducked into her tent.

"Definitely," Thomas said reassuringly, and slipped quietly into his. He got out of his waterlogged jacket and muddy shoes without making a sound. He dried himself off, tiptoed over to his sleeping bag, and stepped right on Stuart Seltzer's hand.

"What's happening?" Stuart asked groggily.

"Shh," Thomas said. "Go back to sleep."

"What are you doing up?" Stuart whispered.

"I had a little adventure," Thomas said.

"Tell," Stuart demanded. So Thomas told Stuart the story of the ghost, complete with crashing branches, flashes of lightning, and a craggy mountain reaching up to the sky.

"Great story," Stuart said as he rolled over in his sleeping bag and tried to go back to sleep. "I'll give you ten points for it." He had assumed, of course, that Thomas had made up the entire thing. "Only next time leave out the part about the *Luna fructosa* berries."

"How come?" Thomas asked warily.

"Well, first of all, *Luna fructosa* only grows in Argentina," Stuart said as if anybody in his right mind would know this. "And second of all, it's poisonous. Why would anyone want to put it into pancakes? Unless they wanted to kill someone. That's quite an imagination you have there, Wiggins."

141

"Uh, thanks, Stuart," Thomas said nervously. "I'll have to remember that next time I tell anyone that story. Don't want points off for inaccuracy," he joked as he rolled over.

Thomas's mind was racing. Pop and Mamie were liars. *What else were they?* Thomas wondered. McGrowl had warned him to be on the lookout for people acting strangely on the island. If this wasn't strange behavior, he didn't know what was.

And then Thomas remembered the look on Pop's face when he returned safely with his brown rubber eagle. The real Pop would have looked proud and happy. This Pop looked as if he had just lost his best friend. Thomas pretended to snore and waited for Stuart to fall asleep. And then he sent an urgent telepathic message to McGrowl.

The dog was back on his cushion in the garage, dreaming about his birthday party. He sat bolt upright when he received Thomas's message: *I'm in danger. Smudge is on the island. I need your help. No time to waste.*

McGrowl ran out of the house and went immediately into hyperspeed. His paws barely touched the ground. A squirrel bringing home a few nuts for the long winter ahead saw the blur on the road and assumed it was a cloud of dust.

In a matter of seconds, McGrowl stood, panting, at the edge of Lake Wappinger. Devil's Island loomed in the distance, ringed with mist and fog. The dog took a deep breath and plunged headlong into the icy water.

CHAPTER ELEVEN
Midnight Run

Thomas and Violet huddled outside their tents and tried to decide what to do. The rain had returned, but Thomas now had on his poncho and boots. "Pop is Milton Smudge in disguise," Thomas explained. "And Mamie is really Gretchen Bunting. There's no doubt about it."

"Of course," Violet said, her voice rising. "We should have known."

"Quiet," Thomas said. "They're probably listening to us right now."

"Let's just hope they haven't done some-

thing terrible to the real Pop and Mamie,"
Violet whispered.

"We're heading back to Harmony Hill,"
Thomas announced as he led Violet up the
path that they had so recently ascended. "I
bet Smudge is hiding the real Pop and Mamie
up there."

"Think that's why Pop warned us not to go
there?" Violet asked.

"Probably," Thomas said, brushing the rain
from his face. He struggled to keep his foot-
ing on the slippery path. Mud was everywhere.

"We've gotta get there before Smudge and
Bunting," Thomas shouted against the howl-
ing wind.

"What do you think they're up to?" Violet
yelled in return.

"Nothing good," Thomas replied. "There's
something going on up there," Thomas said,
pointing to Harmony Hill. It loomed eerily in

the distance. "And we're gonna get to the bottom of it."

Thomas was right. There was something going on up there. Something big. Harmony Hill wasn't a hill at all. It was a volcano. It had lain dormant for the last three hundred years. If Milton Smudge had his way, it was about to come to life again.

● ●

McGrowl sped effortlessly across the lake, creating a giant wake that sent fish scrambling for cover. He was practically flying now. Water churned under his swiftly moving paws. Geese flying south for the holidays gathered overhead and stared down in awe and wonder, honking their approval.

McGrowl arrived on the island and looked around suspiciously. The evil stranger and his accomplice were somewhere in the area. He could sense their presence as clearly as he felt the driving rain against his haunches. As McGrowl shook himself, water cascaded off his fur. He scanned the beach for signs of the children.

They were nowhere to be seen. He raced toward the campground. *Thomas,* he thought, *where are you, Thomas?* In return he heard nothing but the roar of the wind and the rustling of the trees.

• •

Why isn't he answering me? Thomas wondered as they arrived at the base of the hill. He had been sending McGrowl a series of urgent messages. The dog didn't appear to be receiving any of them.

Violet looked behind her furtively. "What if Pop and Mamie are following us?" she asked.

"Don't you mean Milton Smudge and Gretchen Bunting?" Thomas said grimly.

Smudge and Bunting lay peacefully in their

147

sleeping bags, waiting for the inevitable to occur. Smudge had been concerned, at first, when Thomas's annoying mother had prevented McGrowl from coming on Wilderness Weekend. He needed McGrowl on the island. It was part of his plan.

So Smudge had sent Bunting out, disguised as a ghost, to lure Thomas and Violet into the woods, where he could kidnap them. Surely, McGrowl would come to their rescue then.

But that pathetic Thompson woman had gotten in his way. How Smudge hated her! If Miss Thompson hadn't come upon them in the woods, Thomas and Violet would already be tied up and begging for McGrowl to come save them. *Oh, well,* Smudge thought, *that will happen soon enough.*

● ●

McGrowl circled the campground. He braced himself against the raging storm as wind whipped at his ears and icy drops of rain pelted his face. Using his X-ray vision, he peered into each and every one of the tents. Thomas and Violet were nowhere to be seen.

● ●

Closer and closer the children ventured until they were standing directly at the foot of the enormous volcano. As Thomas eyed it warily, Violet noticed what looked like an opening near the base and hurried over to it. She kneeled on the muddy ground and peered into a small cave. She saw something near the entrance and reached inside to pick it up.

"What's that?" Thomas asked.

"I think I found something," Violet answered. "It's the gingham apron Mamie always wears," she said. The real Pop and Mamie were nearby. They had to be. The two children crawled into the little opening. "Hello, hello!" they yelled.

"Don't worry, we're coming to get you," Thomas shouted. A large rock rumbled effortlessly into place behind him. It sealed the entrance to the little cave, trapping Thomas and Violet inside and plunging them into darkness. Smudge had set a trap for them. And they had walked right into it.

●●●●●●●●●●●●●●●●●●●●●●●●●●●●●●

The evil stranger and his accomplice screamed for joy as they leaped from their sleeping bags. They threw on ponchos and rain hats and hurried out of their tent. Their plan was working like a charm. They had been observing Thomas and Violet from the tiny television Milton Smudge had concealed in a cigar box. A number of carefully placed minicameras had allowed Smudge to monitor Thomas and Violet's every movement.

Thomas was indeed correct. Milton Smudge and his wicked accomplice, Gretchen Bunting, had temporarily stolen the identities of Pop and Mamie. Thomas and Violet were trapped snugly at the base of Harmony Hill, and it would soon be time to put the last phase of their vile and ingenious plan into place.

Four weeks ago, the real Pop and Mamie had been lured to Devil's Island. Smudge had introduced himself to them at the annual Cedar Springs Garden Show. He had pretended to be a botanist from London. He had worn a top hat and a false mustache, and he had perfected a flawless British accent. He was, as he put it, "Jolly close to discovering a rare new species of poison ivy."

If only Pop and Mamie would take him across Lake Wappinger and invest a few hours of their precious time helping him in his quest, "It would do the scientific community heaps of good." Eager to help, the good-natured Pop rushed out immediately to rent a boat.

Two hours later, Smudge had hypnotized

Pop and Mamie and hidden them away in a cave at the base of Harmony Hill. They were unharmed and could remain in a state of suspended animation for up to a month with no ill effects. When awakened, they would remember nothing. Then Smudge and Bunting disguised themselves as Pop and Mamie, assumed their identities, and eagerly waited for Wilderness Weekend to begin.

Smudge and Bunting would travel to Devil's Island in the guise of two of the most beloved people in town. No one would suspect them of a thing. With the help of McGrowl's superpowers, Smudge would harness the destructive forces of the volcano and use it to destroy Cedar Springs.

Smudge loved volcanoes. They unleashed massive chaos. Molten lava could be stopped by nothing, and it destroyed everything in its path. "Control the volcano, and you will control the world," he hissed softly to himself. Smudge put his arms around his waist and gave himself a gentle hug. "Oh, happy day!"

Soon Devil's Island would be buried under a mountain of boiling lava and then Lake Wappinger would be filled with the molten liquid, and eventually so would Cedar Springs. It would only be a matter of time before all of Indiana — and eventually, the world — would be in Smudge's clutches.

After the volcano's previous eruption, millions of tons of rock and debris had settled over the opening and prevented it from erupting again. Only a bionic dog would have the strength to remove the blockage and allow the lava to flow freely once more.

Smudge was so excited about his plan he had disguised himself as a delivery boy and gained entrance to Mrs. Wiggins's kitchen. There he inserted his terrifying warning into McGrowl's fortune cookie.

His plan was working. Neither the meddling Mrs. Wiggins nor the bumbling Miss Thompson — not even Thomas's newfound courage — had been able to stand in Smudge's way for long. Nothing could stop him now.

The dog would be his. And then, the world.

CHAPTER TWELVE
Ring of Fire

Why, McGrowl thought, *is that perfectly delicious-looking steak just sitting there and begging me to eat it?* McGrowl had been searching the area behind the dining tent when he came upon the exciting treat. Drenched and exhausted as he was, McGrowl perked up immediately when he spotted the beautifully prepared meal under a brightly decorated canopy.

Another piece of the evil stranger's plan was falling smoothly into place.

McGrowl didn't realize what was happening

until he had the steak firmly between his teeth and a mighty steel box came crashing down over his head. He heard the familiar buzz of the only thing on earth that could take away his powers — an electromagnet. The box had been lined with a network of negatively charged wires that transported the deadly electrons. Within seconds, McGrowl had been drained of every last one of his super-powers.

A similar electromagnetic field had been installed around Harmony Hill. It had prevented Thomas and McGrowl from communicating telepathically.

Superman had kryptonite, McGrowl had an electromagnetic field. Without it, he could do anything. In its presence, he became the Clark Kent of golden retrievers. Smudge was ecstatic. McGrowl was as weak as a newborn pup. The device had operated brilliantly.

Gretchen Bunting dragged the dog harshly

from his cage. He was so weak he could barely stand. Smudge slipped a special collar around his neck. His accomplice carried a portable electromagnet. Concealed beneath her gingham apron, it was connected to McGrowl's collar through a series of wires inserted through the dog's leash.

"We hope you've enjoyed your stay on the island," the stranger hissed menacingly. He leaned over as he spoke and stared directly into McGrowl's eyes. Milton Smudge still looked like jolly old Pop Wheeler, only now he spoke in a soft, demented whisper.

"We're sorry to say you won't be returning here. You'll be coming to live with us, you lucky dog, you. Milton Smudge and Gretchen Bunting will be your new owners. You will help us take over the world. You won't be happy, at first. You'll miss Thomas and Violet. But you'll get used to us. We're not that bad."

And then Smudge thought for a moment.

"Actually, we are that bad." The corners of his lips turned upward in a hideous grin that revealed rotting yellowed teeth.

If this really is the evil stranger, McGrowl wondered, *why doesn't he smell of formaldehyde?* Instead of the familiar acrid odor, the stranger's breath had a sweet scent that reminded the dog strangely of Christmas.

Cinnamon, McGrowl thought. *Of course!* No wonder he hadn't recognized Smudge immediately. Mamie's famous buns provided a perfect cover for the evil pair's recognizable stench. After assuming the identities of Pop and Mamie, the two began bathing in the aromatic spice. They washed their hair with it. They used it to brush their teeth. Constant exposure to cinnamon had removed every trace of their telltale formaldehyde odor.

Once Smudge, Bunting, and McGrowl arrived at the base of Harmony Hill, Smudge put McGrowl far beneath the ground in an abandoned well on the other side of the volcano. Bunting went to pop some popcorn. Doing really evil things made her ravenously hungry.

Meanwhile, Smudge touched a secret button, and the giant rock that covered the entrance to the cave at the base of the hill rolled back, revealing the cavern where Thomas and Violet had been trapped. Now they were nowhere to be seen.

"Goody, goody," Smudge said, clapping his hands together. The plan was working like a charm.

Thomas and Violet had managed to escape. Or so they thought. Trapped in the little cavern and feeling hopeless, Thomas had reached into his pocket and taken out the magical rock his mother had given him for inspiration. His hands were shaking so hard he dropped it on the ground. The stone caused a trail of sparks when it landed on the rocky surface of the cave. The magical rock was made of flint! There was hope after all.

And then Thomas discovered that his mother had stuffed all of his pockets, including those of his pajamas, with dozens of paper tissues. As she frequently said, "You never know when you'll need a tissue."

Thomas and Violet created torches by using the flint to set the tissues on fire. Then they found a small tunnel that led from the base of the cave to another cavern, deeper inside the volcano. Thomas covered over the entrance to the tunnel with leaves and twigs to prevent Smudge and Bunting from following them.

Once in the second cavern, Thomas was shocked to see the real Pop and Mamie Wheeler. Smudge had placed them there for safekeeping. They stood, motionless, near the wall. Their eyes were tightly shut, and they had peaceful expressions on their faces. Mamie actually appeared to be smiling.

Violet shouted in their ears and tickled them under their chins, but nothing she did was able to break the spell and awaken them.

Despite their efforts to cover their tracks, Smudge was hot on Thomas and Violet's trail. He looked down and spotted a crumpled white tissue on the ground. It had fallen from Thomas's pocket. He reached to pick it up and saw the name Thomas Wiggins neatly sewn into one corner. "Mothers," he muttered to himself. "God bless 'em all."

The discarded tissue told Smudge precisely what he needed to know. The children had disappeared into the tunnel, the entrance to which Thomas had attempted to disguise with twigs and leaves. The discarded tissue pointed directly to it. Smudge felt a glow of self-satisfaction. Thomas and Violet were doing exactly what he had hoped they would. Smudge was off and running.

Thomas and Violet heard him coming. "I wouldn't try that if I were you," Smudge said as they picked up rocks and prepared to hurl them at him. He had easily located their hiding place.

"Why not?" Thomas asked boldly.

"Because I've got that mutt of yours strapped to a giant electromagnet, and I am fully prepared to pull the switch if you don't put down those ridiculous rocks and start behaving yourselves." Then Smudge pulled out a small remote control device and started counting.

"Okay, okay," Thomas said quietly. "We give up."

"What if he's lying?" Violet asked.

"What if he's not?" Smudge replied smugly. The children put down their rocks and did exactly what the evil man told them to do.

Smudge whistled cheerfully as he finished tying Violet and Thomas securely together. By the time he was done, they couldn't move a muscle. He didn't have to tie up Pop and Mamie. They were still hypnotized.

Violet heard the sound of flowing water first. She nudged Thomas. The torrential rain had found its way into their prison through a hole in the wall and was pouring into the cavern at an alarming rate. If it continued, the water would soon be over their heads.

Smudge noticed their worried glances. He smiled sweetly as he prepared to leave the cavern. "Have fun, kids. Six points for whoever drowns first." But Smudge knew they were perfectly safe. McGrowl would come to their rescue and activate the volcano. It was all part of his marvelous plan.

Meanwhile, McGrowl struggled vainly on the opposite side of the volcano. He lay strapped to an enormous electromagnet at the bottom of the abandoned well. The magnet emitted a small but steady current of deadly rays — just enough to keep McGrowl's superpowers safely in check. He strained feebly against the chains that wound around his weakened body. He didn't even have the energy to bark.

McGrowl was separated from Thomas and Violet by thousands of tons of rock and debris that held back an ocean of molten lava. In order to rescue the children, he would have to tunnel through to them, allowing the volcano to erupt, unleashing mass destruction on the inhabitants of Cedar Springs. If he didn't . . . McGrowl wouldn't even let himself think of the consequences. The evil duo rushed outside to watch the drama unfold.

Milton Smudge and Gretchen Bunting pulled up folding chairs and found a comfortable spot a few hundred yards away from the volcano. Smudge rubbed his hands together gleefully, pulled out his remote control device, and gave it a flick. The chains that bound

McGrowl dropped to the floor. The whir of the electromagnet ground to a halt. The dog leaped up. In a moment, McGrowl could feel the energy pulsing through his mighty frame as his powers were restored.

With his X-ray vision, McGrowl determined the exact location of Thomas and Violet. With his superhearing, he heard Thomas cry, "Help, help, somebody help!" The water had reached his neck. Violet had to stand on her tiptoes to keep from drowning as the water rose higher and higher. The real Pop and Mamie continued to smile, oblivious to the danger they were in.

Smudge sat back in his chair and waited for the fun to begin. He pulled out a bag of Bunting's freshly buttered popcorn.

McGrowl raced frantically toward the sound of Thomas's voice. The boy's cries for help were becoming more and more faint. The water had risen above his mouth, and as he screamed the water rushed in and garbled his words. Violet was too busy holding her breath to make a sound.

McGrowl fought his way desperately forward. Using his massive strength, he ripped through the volcano's core with his teeth and his paws as easily as if it were papier-mâché. His paws moved so fast they sent off sparks, and still he continued to dig.

Hold on, he thought desperately, and hoped that his message would reach Thomas.

"More popcorn," Gretchen Bunting said as she grabbed for the bag.

"You didn't say please," Smudge replied, and threw the rest of the popcorn onto the ground. "Oh, no, it spilled," he taunted. "No more for you. Too bad!"

"You're a big fat pig," the evil woman retaliated.

"Sticks and stones, sticks and stones,"

Smudge cried, and began picking up handfuls of popcorn and throwing it at Bunting.

"I hate you," Bunting screamed, and attempted to throw the popcorn back at Smudge. Although the evil duo shared a wide variety of similar interests that ranged from taking candy from babies to universal domination, Gretchen Bunting often wondered whether she had chosen a satisfactory partner in crime. How would they ever rule the world together? They could barely stand the sight of each other.

Suddenly, a shower of sparks and debris shot out from the crater at the top of the volcano, accompanied by a deafening roar. Smudge and Bunting watched in awe. Their plan was unfolding beautifully. In a few more seconds, a full-scale eruption would occur. A cloud of ominous black smoke began billowing into the sky. The roaring grew louder.

McGrowl came crashing through the rocky wall and reached Thomas and Violet just in time. He untied them with lightning speed and dragged them out of the cavern to safety. They lay on the grass, gasping for breath, exhausted and frightened but very much alive. Next, McGrowl raced back and retrieved the real Pop and Mamie.

With less than a minute to spare, he began tunneling back into the heart of the volcano. He had to stop the flow of lava before it destroyed Devil's Island, Cedar Springs, and everyone in both places. It was a brave decision, and a dangerous one.

Smudge and Bunting watched nervously. This was definitely not part of the plan. What if McGrowl actually prevented the eruption? Even worse, what if he ended up roasted and charred at the bottom of the volcano?

They needed the bionic dog's help if they were to succeed in their goal of conquering the world. Without McGrowl, Milton Smudge and Gretchen Bunting were evil. But they weren't omnipotent. And they knew it.

McGrowl raced toward the flow of blinding-hot molten lava that was bubbling up from deep within the volcano's core. His fur was singed from the heat, and his ears ached from the deafening roar of the approaching on-slaught. Yet he didn't hesitate for a moment.

McGrowl turned his back and started shov-eling rock and sand toward the lava with his bionic hind legs. He strained and struggled with every molecule in his miraculous body until the pads on his paws were raw and his beautiful golden coat had turned a dusty gray. And still he kept shoveling. He didn't stop until the lava's path was blocked and the volcano's deafening roar grew quiet.

One last belch of blackened smoke sig-naled the end of the eruption. The volcano was once again dormant. McGrowl had saved

Devil's Island and Cedar Springs from certain disaster. No one but Thomas and Violet would ever know about his magnificent accomplishment.

But where was McGrowl? Thomas held his breath. Surely, in a moment, he would emerge triumphant from the volcano. He had to. He was McGrowl, the bionic dog. Nothing could harm him. Still, Thomas waited. Violet thought she saw the wisp of a furry tail beginning to emerge. It turned out to be nothing but smoke and ashes.

Another few seconds slowly ticked by. Thomas looked sadly at his watch. What seemed like an hour turned out to be a minute. Yet his furry friend had still not arrived, wagging his tail and begging to be patted.

Thomas was about to give up hope when McGrowl flew back out of the volcano and rushed over to receive dozens of pats and hugs. Thomas let out a whoop of joy.

"Nobody make a move," said Smudge.

Thomas looked around and saw a badly singed but very much alive Milton Smudge and Gretchen Bunting sitting on their folding chairs and aiming a portable electromagnetic device right at McGrowl's head. It whirred loudly. "Give us the dog, and nobody gets hurt," Smudge announced calmly.

Thomas had learned how to deal with bullies. Sometimes you had to fight back. Without a second thought, he hurled his magical rock at the electromagnet in Smudge's hand. It struck a damaging blow right at the core of the transmission element. All whirring ceased immediately. "Uh-oh," Smudge said, and he and Bunting started to get up. "Freeze," Thomas yelled, "or I'll sic McGrowl on you."

Suddenly, one last chunk of blazing lava flew out of the volcano and landed on Smudge and Bunting, covering them in a cloud of thick black smoke. McGrowl turned around and waved his tail mightily. In a few seconds, the smoke had cleared.

Thomas looked over at the place where Smudge and Bunting had just been sitting. All he saw was a pair of severely singed and empty folding chairs. On the seat of each, a pile of glowing ashes smoldered.

Had the evil duo been incinerated? Were they nothing more than a pile of cinders? Or had they managed to escape?

Thomas went over to look at the chairs more closely and discovered his magical rock. McGrowl wagged his tail to cool it off, and Thomas popped it right back into his pocket.

Just then, the real Pop and Mamie Wheeler woke up and wandered over to Thomas and Violet as if nothing the slightest bit unusual had happened. They yawned and stretched as if they had just woken up from a long nap, which, in a way, they had.

The loud noise of the eruption had awakened them. Fortunately, Smudge had given them a posthypnotic suggestion. When he put them into the trance, he told them that if they woke up, they would think it was the middle of Wilderness Weekend and would continue with their activities as if nothing had happened.

"Bedtime, campers," Pop exclaimed, and then he and Mamie hurried back to their tent and tried to get a little sleep.

"Good night, McGrowl," Violet said, and shook his paw gratefully.

"You were amazing, McGrowl," Thomas said as he leaned down to hug the dog.

McGrowl sent Thomas a telepathic message. He told him that he was amazing, too, and he thanked Thomas for all of his help. He couldn't have succeeded without his boy. Together, they had saved Cedar Springs.

"I guess that means we're partners, aren't we, fella," Thomas told McGrowl.

"Can I be a partner, too?" Violet asked.

"Of course you can," Thomas answered. And then Thomas and Violet went back to their tents, and McGrowl raced home to 27 Walnut Grove Avenue. He was fast asleep on his cushion when dawn broke and Miss Pooch opened her little eyes. She couldn't imagine why McGrowl's coat was such a mess. It had looked perfectly fine the night before.

CHAPTER THIRTEEN
Snake in the Grass

"Go, Brown Team, go!" fifteen excited campers cheered. Behind by four points, the Brown Team had a chance to get ahead in the last and most difficult event of Wilderness Weekend, if only they could find a snake. Any snake. Not a difficult request for a nature competition that had, so far, required the children to locate a chameleon, a hummingbird, and a four-leaf clover.

If the Browns could find the snake before the Greens, they would be declared the winners. With ten minutes to go and not a snake in sight, the Browns started poking around a boggy area near the edge of the lake. The very thing that Miss Thompson, the Brown Team's faculty adviser, had been trying to avoid all weekend long was the very thing that would bring victory to her team.

Lewis Musser had ordered his team to look under canoes. "Snakes," he told the Greens, "hang out in canoes. Everybody knows that." Lewis didn't know very much about nature.

So far, neither team was having any luck finding a snake. The desperation level was rising. Friendly cheers, urging each team to "Win with honor, win with grace, never throw pies in the other team's face!" had descended to angry cheers urging the campers to "Stomp them to the ground, we don't mess around, pound, pound, pound!"

Suddenly, a cheer erupted from the Brown Team. A snake had been spotted. As the children raced to catch it, Miss Thompson ran madly in the other direction. "Snake, snake!" she screamed. No one paid any attention. Then she stumbled and disappeared into a hole. Her team rushed to her rescue.

Miss Thompson was shrieking hysterically. She had encountered the newest residence of the little family of gophers. They had just unpacked their last belongings when Miss Thompson ran across their freshly tunneled area and fell straight through the weakened ground.

As everyone ran to help her, she stood trembling and covered with mud. "I'm perfectly fine. Pay no attention to me, campers," she said nervously.

Just then, Esther Mueller spotted a harmless little green garter snake — on Miss Thompson's head. She nudged Violet, who nudged Stuart Seltzer, and pretty soon all the

Browns were cheering and yelling, "We won, we won!" Just spotting the snake meant victory for the Brown Team.

Even Miss Thompson joined in, although she didn't know what all the fuss was about. No one had the heart to tell her about the snake that was sitting on her hat and looking around eagerly. It seemed to be enjoying all the attention.

And then Miss Thompson became so caught up in the excitement she took her hat in her hands and threw it into the air joyously. The snake didn't seem to mind. It and the hat flew through the air and landed in a big puddle. The little snake slithered away, unharmed.

All the while, two pair of eyes stared out from the woods and watched the happy campers. Singed and bruised but very much alive, the evil stranger and his accomplice would return with a better plan. "Next time, next time," Milton Smudge said to himself as he limped away.

At last, the campers were loaded onto the bus. Everyone sang "Now the Day Is Over," although night had yet to arrive. Thomas and Violet fell asleep the minute they reached their seats and didn't wake up until the bus pulled into Thomas's driveway.

McGrowl came racing out to greet the children. He barked and wagged his tail and pretended he hadn't just seen both Thomas and Violet the night before.

McGrowl was followed closely by Miss Pooch. Violet was amazed that the bullwawa came when called and seemed a lot calmer. When Violet put on her leash, she didn't try to run away for a second. Violet's parents had just returned from the wedding. They would be pleased to see what a positive influence McGrowl had on their pet.

As Violet and Miss Pooch turned to leave,

McGrowl walked over to say good-bye. He didn't seem to mind a bit when Miss Pooch gave him a big lick on his nose.

"Bye, McGrowl. Bye, Thomas," Violet called as she headed across the street to her house. "See you in the morning."

McGrowl would miss the little dog and planned to stop by the Schnayersons after dinner to take her for a walk.

Then Mrs. Wiggins rushed out to greet Thomas.

"Let me get a good look at you," she said, wiping her hands on her apron. "On second thought, maybe I better not. What did they do to you, Thomas Wiggins, dip you in mud?" She laughed and then she hugged him tightly as they walked into the kitchen. "I don't care," she said. "You're home, and that's all that matters."

Soon a freshly scrubbed Thomas sat at the kitchen table while his mother put the finishing touches on a delicious welcome-home meal. Turkey with all the trimmings was roasting in the oven, and a sweet potato pie was cooling on the counter. McGrowl sat on the floor beside Thomas's feet. It felt good to be home at last.

"Let me ask you something," Mrs. Wiggins said after Thomas had described the ghost story and the canoe race and all the singing and cheering. He neglected to mention the eagle's nest and the erupting volcano. "Did you make any new friends?"

"Lots. I'm having a sleepover with Ralph Sidell next weekend. And Stuart Seltzer invited me to his birthday party," said Thomas.

"Isn't that wonderful," Mrs. Wiggins said. She had worried all weekend about her decision not to allow McGrowl on the trip. She smiled as she beat an especially persistent lump out of the gravy. "I'm so glad."

"You know, Mom," Thomas said, "there are times when you just have to do things all on your own."

"Aren't there, though," Mrs. Wiggins agreed.

"But there are other times when you need a friend to help you out. And sometimes it's hard to tell which is which."

Mrs. Wiggins felt a catch in her throat. Her eyes were moist. "I'm proud of you, Thomas," she said.

"Thanks, Mom," Thomas answered. "But I'm not doing anything special, I'm just growing up."

McGrowl's tail thumped loudly on the floor in agreement. Thomas reached down and patted him on the top of his noble head. McGrowl rested a reassuring paw on Thomas's foot and sent him a message. *Good boy*, McGrowl said. *Good boy*.

Thomas sent one in return. *You, too, McGrowl. You, too.*

Mr. Wiggins would return from work soon, and Roger had agreed to skip basketball practice tonight to attend Thomas's special dinner.

Tomorrow was another day. There would more fun, more surprises, and more mashed potatoes. There would be more birthdays. And certainly, although neither McGrowl nor Thomas was aware of it yet, there would be more visits from the evil strangers.

Thomas put his hand in his pocket and grasped the magical rock. It had kept him and McGrowl safe from harm. Hopefully, it would again, the next time they needed it. Which would be a lot sooner than Thomas could possibly have imagined.

Bob Balaban is a respected producer, director, writer, and actor. He produced and costarred in Robert Altman's Oscar®- and Golden Globe–winning film *Gosford Park*, which was named Best British Film of 2001 at the British Academy Awards. He appeared in *Close Encounters of the Third Kind*, *Absence of Malice*, *Deconstructing Harry*, *Waiting for Guffman*, *Ghost World*, *The Mexican*, and *A Mighty Wind*, among many other films, and appeared on *Seinfeld* several times as the head of NBC. Bob produced and directed the feature films *Parents* and *The Last Good Time*, which won best film and best director awards at the Hamptons International Film Festival. Bob lives in New York with his wife, writer Lynn Grossman, and his daughters, Hazel and Mariah. At the moment, he is canine-less, but he is looking forward to a close encounter with his own actual dog, not just one of the literary kind.

Adventure Abounds in These Awesome Series...

Emily Rodda

An epic fight against forces of darkness.

Gordon Korman

ISLAND

The rules have just been swept away...

Chris Archer

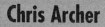

The TREASURE is real. And so is the DANGER.

BOYT1